the Princess Revolt

Unraveled

the Princess Revolt

By Cathy O'Neill

Aladdin

New York   London   Toronto   Sydney   New Delhi

ALADDIN

An imprint of Simon & Schuster Children's Publishing Division

1230 Avenue of the Americas, New York, New York 10020

First Aladdin hardcover edition March 2022

Text copyright © 2022 by Cathy O'Neill

Jacket illustration copyright © 2022 by Sarah Mensinga

All rights reserved, including the right of reproduction in whole or in part in any form.

ALADDIN and related logo are registered trademarks of Simon & Schuster, Inc.

For information about special discounts for bulk purchases, please contact Simon & Schuster Special Sales at 1-866-506-1949 or business@simonandschuster.com.

The Simon & Schuster Speakers Bureau can bring authors to your live event.

For more information or to book an event contact the Simon & Schuster Speakers Bureau at 1-866-248-3049 or visit our website at www.simonspeakers.com.

Jacket designed by Karin Paprocki

Interior designed by Mike Rosamilia

The text of this book was set in Bodoni Egyptian Pro.

Manufactured in the United States of America 0222 FFG

2 4 6 8 10 9 7 5 3 1

Library of Congress Cataloging-in-Publication Data

Names: O'Neill, Cathy, author.

Title: The princess revolt / by Cathy O'Neill.

Description: First Aladdin hardcover edition. | New York : Aladdin, 2022. | Series: Unraveled | Summary: Shortly after her thirteenth birthday, Cia Anderson discovers that fairy-tale princesses are real, they live in New York, and they really want the spell placed on Cia when she was a baby to stop disrupting their happily ever afters.

Identifiers: LCCN 2021017481 (print) | LCCN 2021017482 (ebook) | ISBN 9781534497740 (hc) | ISBN 9781534497764 (ebook)

Subjects: CYAC: Characters in literature—Fiction. | Fairy tales—Fiction. | Magic—Fiction. | Middle schools—Fiction. | Schools—Fiction. | LCGFT: Novels.

Classification: LCC PZ7.1.C6457 Pr 2022 (print) | LCC PZ7.1.C6457 (ebook) | DDC [Fic]—dc23

LC record available at https://lccn.loc.gov/2021017481

LC ebook record available at https://lccn.loc.gov/2021017482

For Kate, Maeve, Evie, and Rose

the Princess Revolt

Chapter 1

IT HAD BEEN ELEVEN NIGHTS SINCE I'D SLEPT.

I don't mean I'd tossed and turned in bed and had difficulty falling, or staying, asleep.

I had not slept. At all.

I'd been awake for the past two hundred and sixty-four hours. I'd read on the American Pediatric Association website—not a site that I would usually visit, but when you're awake at three a.m., these are the things you find yourself doing—that the recommended amount of sleep for thirteen-year-olds is between eight and ten hours a night. As a thirteen-year-old girl who

had gotten no sleep for two hundred and sixty-four hours, I had found this information quite disturbing.

The thing was, though, that I felt absolutely fine. I'd been to enough sleepovers to know what the day after not getting enough sleep was supposed to feel like, and I didn't feel that way. I didn't feel grumpy or sluggish or even the tiniest bit tired. I hadn't as much as yawned in the past ten days. If anything, I felt more awake than usual. In the past few nights, I had:

- ✔ Reread all the Harry Potter and Percy Jackson books.
- ✔ Checked and rechecked all my homework.
- ✔ Finished a paper on the digestive system that wasn't due until the end of the semester.
- ✔ Reorganized the clothes in my closet by type, then material, then color, then back to type.
- ✔ Watched eight seasons of *Friends* and most of *Gilmore Girls*.

✔ Taught myself how to moonwalk.

✔ Tried—and failed—to teach myself how to apply eyeliner.

✔ Learned how to French, fish tail, and Dutch braid my hair.

You can get a *lot* done between the hours of ten p.m. and seven a.m. when no one is telling you to get off the internet (my parents) or trying to get you to watch funny cat videos (my little brother, Riley).

Based off a quick *How long can a person stay awake?* Google search, I'd learned that I was now just a few hours away from breaking the record, which was set by a high school student named Randy Gardner, who, in 1964, in a total last-minute, let's-get-out-of-homework move, decided that going without sleep would be his science fair entry.

Things didn't work out so well for Randy. After four days without sleep, he couldn't remember how to play chess, and by day six, snakes and ladders was too difficult for him. Ever since I'd read about Randy's board game wipeout, I'd been challenging my dad to a chess match every night. And every evening I'd beaten him. Although this—and my shockingly good grades—made me worry less about the state of my brain, I wasn't so sure about the rest of me. So, I'd insisted that Dad, who didn't believe me and thought I was just experiencing long and hyperrealistic dreams, take me to the doctor.

I was scheduled to meet with Dr. Loomis before school in the morning. I glanced at my phone. It was five a.m. In just a few hours I'd be talking to someone who'd have answers about what was happening to me. Finally. Other than finding out about the recommended sleep cycles of teens, the internet had been useless. I'd spent tens of hours online reading about all the things that were *not* happening to me, like not being as smart as usual (see Randy Gardner's chess playing) and bone-crushing tiredness.

The only person I told besides Dad was my best friend, Romy, who went straight to the Dracula option. Mom was halfway across the world on a tiny island that had no cell service, so I couldn't tell her about what was going on. And even if Mom had been here, I wasn't sure I'd tell her anything. Mom overreacted about things—well, maybe not *things*, but she overreacted about me—and I was afraid of what she'd say and do if I told her that I no longer needed to sleep. Dad's reaction was understandable, though—I did look absolutely fine (same medium-length curly brown hair, same palish skin with a smatter of freckles, and same hazel eyes), and my chess playing was outstanding. I'd won every game. Romy believed me straightaway because, as she said, why would I make something like this up? We had discussed the Dracula possibility during a sleepover at her house—that's the kind of friend Romy is; she suspected I might be a vampire, and she still let me share her bedroom—and then ruled it out. I hadn't developed any strange, bloody cravings, and I didn't sleep at all, unlike vampires who sleep during the day and roam about at night looking for necks to bite.

I was sure Dr. Loomis wouldn't want to chat about bloodsucking creatures. She was a doctor. She'd have to know why I had stopped needing to sleep, and she'd have answers. I had just a few more hours to wait until I found out why I, unlike every human being on the planet—according to the American Sleep Association—was able to function normally without any sleep.

A noise from Riley's room made me poke my head

in—I sort of hoped he was awake; it got boring some-times, just hanging out on my own hour after hour, night after night—but he was fast asleep. He must have been dreaming. I sat down on the comfy chair beside his bed and listened to the sounds coming from the street below. We lived in Brooklyn, so even in the deepest, darkest part of the night, there were noises outside: car doors closing, the hum of garbage trucks, and distant sounds of ambu-lances and fire sirens.

Riley let out a little burble of laughter and kicked his legs, throwing the covers off. I reached over and put the comforter back on top of him. His head was resting on his favorite book, *The Big Book of Outrageous Facts*. He wasn't able to read most of it, but it didn't stop him from quoting it all the time. Just before he'd gone to bed, he'd told me that he'd read there were more saunas than cars in Finland. (I didn't think Riley even knew what a sauna was.) I gently pulled it out from under his head and put it on the bedside table. I noticed that the light coming in from outside the bedroom window was changing from dark to hazy gray. It was almost morning.

I went back to my room and opened my closet, where

I saw a T-shirt that Mom had given me a couple of weeks ago. It said, I AM SMART! I AM STRONG! I CAN DO ANYTHING! (It was ridiculous-looking, but not as bad as the "surprise" Mom had put in my room just before she left for her trip. I was still mad about that.) For a fraction of a second I wondered what John Lee, the boy I liked, would think of it. Could this T-shirt be the conversation opener I'd been looking for? No, definitely not. I'd be better off wearing Riley's Captain Underpants pajamas to school.

I pushed the T-shirt aside and picked out a pale yellow top and jeans. Then I walked downstairs and headed into the kitchen to make breakfast. I was just about ready to flip my French toast when I heard the old floorboards upstairs creaking, letting me know that my dad had gotten out of bed.

I had broken a world record. My twelfth day without sleep had begun.

Chapter 2

B Y THE TIME DAD AND RILEY CAME DOWNSTAIRS, the kitchen table looked like a hotel buffet. Omelets, pancakes, toasted bagels. I'd even sprinkled icing sugar on the French toast. Back when I used to sleep, I'd just grab a granola bar and a banana on my way out the door, but the no-need-for-sleep me was a whiz in the kitchen, whisking and sieving and poaching breakfast to the amazement and delight of my dad and little brother.

"This is great, Cia," said Dad, clinking my glass of orange juice with the bottle of maple syrup. "If you keep this up, I'll have to buy new pants." He patted his stomach, which was straining against his waistband. Dad should have bought new pants about ten pounds ago.

"I want new pants with frogs on them," said Riley, who loved all animals, especially the ones that could fit in his pocket. "Rocket frogs can jump six feet."

Riley slid off his chair and hunkered down onto his ankles. Then he propelled himself across the kitchen. I ran and grabbed his backpack off the floor—I'd just put his lunch and juice box in it—making sure he didn't crash-land on top of it.

The frog facts continued on the drive to Riley's school. It was actually nice to hear about poisonous amphibians instead of thinking about what Dr. Loomis would say when she heard I'd stopped sleeping. I missed Riley's chatter after Dad and I dropped him off and headed for the pediatrician's office. For the rest of the drive, I picked at a hangnail and tried not to think about Dr. Loomis giving me some terrible diagnosis or—and this would be even worse—Dr. Loomis not being able to figure out what was going on with me. What if she insisted that I check in to a lab to be studied? It'd be just me and the guinea pigs.

At the office, Dad and I were shown to the princess

room. All the exam rooms at Dr. Loomis's were decorated with a kid-friendly theme, and Snow White, Sleeping Beauty, and the rest of the gang from the Magic Kingdom gazed down at me from their pictures on the walls. It was the kind of room you'd be excited about if you were six—not so much if you were thirteen. (Though I still liked the Lego/Star Wars room. That one was cool.) I was so happy that Dad was with me and not Mom. Mom would hate the decorations so much, she'd probably ask for us to be moved, or she'd grab a Sharpie and draw mustaches on all the princesses.

Mom hated Disney princesses the way other moms hated sugary nonorganic snacks. It wasn't just Disney princesses, though. Mom hated any stories—especially magical ones—that, in her opinion, showed girls as being weak and helpless. Even though I felt ridiculous sitting here with Rapunzel and Ariel, a part of me was still mad at Mom for not letting me dress up as Belle for Halloween when I was five. All I'd wanted was to wear those gorgeous yellow gloves and the swishy dress that my grandma, Dad's mom, had sent to me—but Mom packed it all up and sent it back, muttering about "one-dimensional twits" and complaining that they were "destroying girls' self-esteem." I still didn't understand why she got so mad. They were just fairy-tale characters.

"So, Cia, what's going on?" said Dr. Loomis, coming in to the room. My name is Boadecia, but fortunately, no one but my family and best friend, Romy, knows that. Everyone calls me Cia. Mom was getting a PhD in mythology when she was pregnant with me and decided to name me after a Celtic warrior queen who—if legends are to be believed—took on the whole Roman army. It's a lot to live up to. She'd wanted to name my brother "Heimdall" after some Norse god, but eight-year-old me told her that it was the ugliest name that I had ever heard. Riley owes me forever for saving him from nicknames like Heimy or, even worse, Heinie.

"I'm not sleeping," I said, feeling my chest tightening as I spoke. I had insisted that Dad take me to the doctor, but now that I was about to tell someone other than my dad and Romy about my totally weird situation, I felt nervous. What if Dr. Loomis told me that not needing to sleep was a symptom of some horrific, super-rare disease? That would be terrifying. Or that somehow I'd accidentally done something mortifying that was causing my no-sleep condition. I thought about T.J. Sullivan, a boy in my grade, who—when he went to the school nurse because of a nosebleed—found out that he'd had a popcorn kernel stuck up his nasal cavity for months. Some students thought that it was hilarious; others thought that it was disgusting; but either way, it was all anyone talked about for a couple of days. I didn't want students comparing me to the kid who had stuck popcorn up his nose.

"I haven't slept for days," I continued. *In fact, I've broken the world record.*

"Not sleeping for days," confirmed Dr. Loomis thoughtfully, smoothing down her hair. "Well, that's not good." She gave me a knowing look and a nod that seemed reassuring, as if she'd heard this complaint hundreds of times before.

I felt my shoulders sag with relief. Maybe Dr. Loomis had loads of teenage patients who didn't need to sleep. A tiny seed of hope opened up inside me. Maybe what I was going through was normal.

"A lot of kids your age have issues with their sleep. Are you waking up during the night?" She took off her glasses and cleaned them with the hem of her white coat.

"No." I shook my head. "I can't fall asleep."

"So, you're having trouble falling asleep?" she asked, tapping her pen on the top of her laptop.

"I can't fall asleep," I repeated. "At all."

"So, how many hours of sleep are you getting on most nights?"

I felt a flash of frustration and despair. Was Dr. Loomis just ignoring what I'd said? I'd told her that I couldn't fall asleep. And if I couldn't fall asleep, then obviously I couldn't sleep. How could I be getting any hours of sleep if I couldn't fall asleep in the first place?

"I'm not . . . ," I began. I paused, trying to keep my voice steady. I felt like I might start shouting. I glanced over at Dad, who was looking at me with a mixture of confusion and concern on his face.

"I'm not sleeping at all," I said firmly. "I know it sounds impossible, but I don't need to sleep anymore."

Dad inhaled deeply and shifted his position in the chair.

"I close my eyes, but . . ." I stopped, staring down at the floor. I didn't want to see Dad's and Dr. Loomis's reactions, but I had to say it. "I haven't slept for eleven nights."

Dr. Loomis laughed so loudly, I looked up. "That's just not possible," she said, an expression of amusement on her face. She looked at me and then at Dad, then back at me.

"I've told her that," said Dad, leaning forward in his chair.

"But I haven't slept for eleven days," I snapped, feeling angry about Dr. Loomis's burst of laughter and the *Aren't-kids-just-wacky?* glance she and Dad had exchanged.

"Okay," said Dr. Loomis soothingly, raising both her palms. "Let's just take a look, Cia." She scooted her stool toward the examination table. "How do you feel? Have you missed school because of this?"

"I haven't missed any school." I sighed, sinking back into the chair. The rush of adrenaline I'd felt at not being believed was fading, and the nervous feeling was coming back. I didn't like the curious way Dr. Loomis was looking at me. The line between her eyebrows was deepening as she creased her face into an expression of confusion.

"Okay, Cia," she said, standing up. "Let's just check on

a few things." She pointed toward the examination table. I walked over to it and hopped on, my legs swinging over the side. Dr. Loomis did the usual well-check things—blood pressure cuff on the arm, hammer thing on the knees and elbows, fingers on the wrist, stethoscope on the back, and finally, "Follow the tiny flashlight with your eyes." Then she added a few things that I'd never done before, like standing on one leg with my eyes closed and pushing a fist against the palm of her hand. When she finished, she took a step back and put her hands in the pockets of her white lab coat.

"You're totally healthy, Cia," she said, smiling. "All your vital signs are excellent. You're a very healthy young woman."

I nodded. That was good news, right? I didn't have a super-rare, scary disease, and none of the bad things that had happened to poor Randy were happening to me.

"You're not sleep-deprived at all," continued Dr. Loomis as she reached over to grab her laptop from the desk.

"But I am," I said, my voice cracking a bit. "I *am* sleep-deprived. I haven't slept for days. I haven't slept for eleven days!"

"Cia, if that were true," said Dr. Loomis softly, looking up from the keyboard she was typing on, "if you hadn't slept for eleven days, you'd have an erratic heartbeat, your blood pressure would be sky-high, your breathing would be labored, and you wouldn't be able to keep track of this conversation."

I nodded. I already knew all this. A couple of hours on the American Sleep Association website had gotten me up to speed, and Dad relayed the same facts to me every time I told him that I'd stopped needing to sleep.

"If you weren't getting enough sleep, you'd be hallucinating. You'd be having delusions . . . seeing things that aren't there."

Seeing things that aren't there. I'd read about this online, how sleep deprivation could cause hallucinations, and I'd actually, very briefly, worried that it was happening to me. A couple of nights ago, I'd seen something in our backyard that didn't seem real. Something that didn't seem possible. I'd been reading in the chair in Riley's room, and I saw, or sensed, movement outside his window. When I looked outside, in our tiny backyard there was a creature as big as a person crouched on the ground. At first I'd thought it was a long-legged bird, like a crane, its white feathers glowing in the moonlight, but then it took flight, and as it flew off, it looked more like a woman. A woman with wings. She actually reminded me a bit of Mrs. Talen, my history teacher. Same hint of a double chin and messy gray hair.

I knew what I'd seen was real, though. It hadn't been a hallucination. My stomach seized up at the thought of what I'd found in the backyard the next morning. A white feather as long as my arm. It had freaked me out so much that I had just wanted to forget about the whole thing. I didn't tell anyone about this flying Mrs. Talen–like creature, as if not talking about it could mean it hadn't happened.

Pushing the image away, I tuned back in to what Dr. Loomis was saying.

"So, Cia, you look and act like someone who is getting sleep. Medically speaking, you look great."

Dr. Loomis turned to my dad.

"Would you mind giving us a couple of minutes on our own?" she asked.

"Sure," said Dad, giving me a little smile as he got

up and walked toward the door. He closed it carefully behind him.

Dr. Loomis sat down in the chair my dad had just vacated.

"Cia, how is everything at home? Your dad mentioned your mom's been away for a few weeks. . . ."

"Yeah . . . ," I said, wondering why Dr. Loomis was asking me about Mom. And why did Dad have to leave the room for this part of the conversation? What else was she going to ask me?

"It can be very difficult when a parent is away . . . ," Dr. Loomis continued.

I sighed, starting to see where Dr. Loomis might be going with her line of questioning. Did she think that I was so upset about my mom being gone that I was pretending I didn't need to sleep? That was ridiculous. For one thing, I wasn't upset. I was used to Mom being away on trips when she was researching a new book, though I didn't like it when she went somewhere that was so remote—like the Solomon Islands, where she was now—that I wasn't able to talk to her on the phone. And, aside from that, why would I ever pretend that I didn't need to sleep?

"It's really okay," I said. I hated the sympathetic way Dr. Loomis was looking at me, as if she thought I was about to burst into tears. "Anyway, she'll be back on Friday."

"You must be missing her, though," probed Dr. Loomis.

"Yeah." I nodded, saying what I thought Dr. Loomis wanted to hear. But the truth was that I hadn't really missed Mom. I'd been trying not to think about her because I was feeling awful about the way I'd shouted at her the night before she left. And it was also really nice to get a break from her motivational mania. Not just because I wasn't going to open my closet and find more I CAN DO ANYTHING! T-shirts that were destined to never leave my room; it was also because as long as Mom was away I wouldn't have to worry about her putting inspirational quotes in my backpack. She'd started doing that last month. Two of them had fallen out during math class a couple of weeks ago, and Roger Wu, who never missed a chance to say or do something to embarrass another person, had picked them up and bellowed out the contents while waving them over his head. "'CIA, YOU ARE STRONG AND POWERFUL! SHINE SO BRIGHTLY

THAT OTHERS CAN SEE THEIR WAY OUT OF THE DARK!'"

Our math teacher, Mr. Martinez, had told Roger to shut up, but everyone in the class still turned around to stare at me. It was awful.

"What about school?" continued Dr. Loomis. "Is everything okay there?"

Everything really was okay at school. I had the best of all best friends and some cool teachers, and most of the kids in my grade were nice. Everything was fine except for the fact that I didn't need to sleep anymore.

"What does school have to do with me not sleeping?" I could hear a desperate whine in my voice. The thing was, I *was* desperate. I'd thought Dr. Loomis would have answers, and all she had so far were questions. I was hoping she'd say that recent medical studies were showing that adolescents need far less sleep than doctors had thought, or that a growing number of teenagers were functioning perfectly on no sleep for extended periods. Or something like that.

Not this.

"Look, Cia, you are an intelligent girl. . . . You must

understand that you telling me you haven't slept *at all* for the past eleven days is like telling me that you can hold your breath for an hour or levitate off that chair or practice telekinesis. . . ."

"Moving things with my mind?" I clarified, feeling a little bubble of fear and excitement in the pit of my stomach.

"Exactly," said Dr. Loomis, smiling. "And that is not physically possible. Just like it's not physically possible for a human being to get no sleep for eleven days and be able to function as normal."

She shook her head and laughed in a friendly way that made it clear that she wasn't laughing at me; she was laughing at the thought that anyone could go without sleep for eleven days and function normally.

But functioning normally without any sleep was exactly what I was doing. I swallowed, pushing down the feeling of uneasiness that was building up inside me.

"Cia," continued Dr. Loomis, "if you could actually function without sleep, you'd be superhuman."

"Superhuman," I repeated under my breath.

Was not needing to sleep a superpower? An image of Superman popped into my brain. He was followed by

Spider-Man. Captain America and the Hulk. Did those guys not need to sleep? Now that I thought about it, I'd never seen a movie or read a comic book where the superhero slept. What did that mean? My heart started pounding as my brain raced through the possibilities. What if other superpowers were about to kick in? What if not needing to sleep was just the start? Of . . . Of what? No, this was too much. I told myself to stop being ridiculous. There was no way I was becoming a superhero because superheroes weren't actually real.

I groaned.

"Now, Cia," said Dr. Loomis, giving me a sharp look, "there is nothing to worry about. You are absolutely fine. Most likely, you're just having trouble falling asleep. Let's have you try melatonin for a few nights and see if that helps."

"Okay," I said. I just wanted to get out of her office. I was more freaked out now than I had been when I came in. This morning I'd just been worried about all the damage that sleep deprivation might be causing me; now I was worried that I was becoming some kind of mutant. "Thanks. I'll take the melatonin."

"I'll send your dad back in," said Dr. Loomis, rising from the chair. "And don't worry about anything. You're a very healthy young woman."

I waited for Dad, listening to the hum of his conversation with Dr. Loomis on the other side of the closed door. If I was becoming superhuman, it wasn't affecting my hearing. I couldn't make out a word they were saying.

Chapter 3

DAD DIDN'T SAY *I TOLD YOU SO*, BUT I COULD tell by the tone of his voice that he was thinking it. The quieter I am, the more Dad talks, and I hadn't said a word since we'd left Dr. Loomis. As we headed toward my school, I thought about what she had said, and the term "superhuman" kept repeating in my head. Dr. Loomis was wrong. Not being able to sleep didn't make me superhuman. What was so super about it anyway? It wasn't like being able to fly, or being strong enough to pick up a school bus, or being invisible.

I looked out the window and concentrated on the

building we were driving by, just in case I'd developed X-ray vision and hadn't realized it. No, I hadn't. All I could see was the outside of the building. I looked down and focused on the backpack at my feet, willing it to move. It didn't.

I decided to try one more thing. Dad had stopped talking and had a thoughtful look on his face. I stared at him, willing myself to read his mind. I couldn't. I sighed and slumped down into my seat, not sure if I was relieved or disappointed.

An ad played on the car radio, cutting through my thoughts, with a woman gushing about the amazing-ness of Forever Young skin care products. Mom always turned off the radio when it played, telling me that no one should "impose a definition of beauty on anyone else." Sometimes I was pretty sure Mom forgot that I wasn't one of the college students she taught. The ad was just for makeup. What was so terrible about that?

Girls in my grade wore Forever Young products like lip gloss and foundation and mascara to school every day, and Mia Johnson—wielding tweezers and a blush brush like they were magic wands—gave makeup tutorials in the restroom during study hall. It all seemed like a lot of work to me, figuring out what shades to use and what pencil went where, but sometimes I did wonder if I should get in on the action too. Might John Lee actually notice me if—as Mia Johnson claimed—I wore sapphire-blue eyeliner to make my eyes pop?

I zoned back in to Dad talking about all the times he took me to the pediatrician when I was a baby. He's very sentimental. It doesn't take much to set him off down memory lane.

"You hardly even blinked when you got a shot," he continued, expounding on Cia: The Baby Years. "The other babies would scream with fright. But not you. You were such a brave little one."

He glanced over at me and smiled as if being so fat as a baby—I'd seen the photos—that I couldn't feel the needles was a remarkable achievement.

"You didn't sleep much, though," he continued. "You kept us awake every night for the first couple of months."

Now, that was interesting.

"I didn't sleep?" I asked, trying to sound as if I had only the most casual interest in my infant sleep habits. If

Dad thought I was trying to make a connection—which was exactly what I was hoping I could do—between what was happening now and me not sleeping when I was a baby, then he might clam up.

"Took you a few months to get the hang of that," said Dad. "Your mom and I, we were exhausted. I thought we'd just lose it. Your mom got so desperate, she took you to some kind of baby sleep-whisperer." He laughed. "I thought it was ridiculous, a lot of hocus-pocus. But your mom was delighted. Said she'd proved me wrong because you started sleeping through the night afterward."

"After I met a baby-whisperer?" I asked, wanting to make sure I understood precisely what Dad was saying. What was a baby-whisperer?

"Baby *sleep*-whisperer," he clarified, giving me a big wink to show that he still thought it was a lot of hocus-pocus.

Dad stopped the car at the entrance of Hill Country Middle School, my bizarrely named school. Because there were no big hills in Brooklyn. There wasn't even room for any.

I got out of the car, then reached in for my backpack

and threw it over my shoulder. I glanced at the clock on the car dashboard. 9:30 A.M. The bell was about to ring for the end of first period. If I hurried, I'd be able to catch up with Romy before the next class started.

"Love you," shouted Dad, grinning at me as he leaned out the car window.

I winced. I'd told him not to do that. I'd had to tell him to lay off the public hugging, too.

"You'll get a great night's sleep tonight," continued Dad. "I'll pick up some melatonin for you."

"Thanks," I said, turning toward the school, ignoring the cheerful tone in his voice. I knew there was about as much a chance of me getting a great night's sleep as there was of Mrs. Everley, the school principal, breaking into a tap dance in the school cafeteria.

I ran across the crosswalk, eager to get inside and out of the thick, damp mist that had suddenly descended over the street and the school. I could barely see two feet ahead of me. I shivered in my T-shirt and jeans, basically the same outfit I wore almost every day. Who could have expected freezing temperatures in May?

I had almost reached the end of the crosswalk when

I looked up and saw a deer standing in front of—and blocking—the doors to the school. I stopped. It might as well have been a unicorn. There were no deer in the wild in Brooklyn. Raccoons and squirrels and maybe even bats, but no deer. It was huge—or maybe it just looked huge because of its massive antlers—and it was looking *right at me.*

The deer flared its nostrils before bowing its head. I knew what was coming, jumping out of its path just as it rushed past me. One of the antlers ripped my T-shirt as I dodged and made for the school's double doors. I opened them and ran inside, slamming them behind me.

"You're late," said Mrs. Brennan, the school reception-ist, peering at me from behind her glasses. Mrs. Brennan was not a woman to be trifled with. She had no sense of humor or imagination or fondness for anyone under the age of thirty.

"There's a deer . . ." I gasped, trying to catch my breath as I looked back outside through the glass doors. But the deer, along with the mist that had covered the parking lot, was gone.

"A deer?" said Mrs. Brennan, raising one eyebrow and

looking at me as if I'd told her a spaceship had just landed in the parking lot. "Is that why you're late?"

"No," I said, handing her the note from Dr. Loomis's office.

My hand was shaking, either from the shock of my encounter with the deer or from the death stare Mrs. Brennan was giving me.

"I'd better get to class," I said, taking off down the hallway.

"DON'T RUN!" yelled Mrs. Brennan.

I slowed down to a fast walk but sped up when I saw Romy standing at the lockers. I needed to tell her about the morning I'd had. Romy's reaction to me not sleeping was super supportive and (sort of) scientific. During my first no-sleep week, one night she'd called me on the hour, every hour, from ten p.m. to six a.m. to check on how I was doing and to confirm—for both of us—that I wasn't nodding off. The next day she was exhausted but fired up about figuring out why I didn't need to sleep anymore. She'd been nearly as excited as I'd been to hear what Dr. Loomis would have to say.

Romy had the locker next to mine. She was standing

beside it reading *Romeo and Juliet*—the auditions for the spring play were that afternoon, and Romy was hoping to be cast as Juliet.

"Hi," I said, throwing my backpack down on the ground.

"So, how did it go?" gasped Romy, wheeling around to face me.

"It was..." I paused, taking in Romy's eager expression. I didn't know where to start. My encounter with the deer? Dr. Loomis's comments about being superhuman? The discovery that Mom had taken me to a sleep-whisperer when I was a baby?

"What did the doctor say?" asked Romy excitedly.

I lowered my voice, even though it wasn't likely our conversation could be heard over the chaos of locker doors opening and closing and the roar of fifty students chatting. "She didn't believe me."

"Oh, c'mon!" said Romy, putting her book in the locker and slamming the door shut. "That is ridiculous. How could she not believe you? What . . . Did she think you were just making it up?" Her brown eyes flashed with annoyance.

"I guess so. Or just exaggerating." I sighed. "She said that if I actually didn't need to sleep anymore, I'd be . . ." I stopped. I thought about how Romy had suggested that I eat raw meat to check if there was anything to the vampire theory. If I told her about Dr. Loomis's comment that not needing to sleep was a superhuman ability, she'd want to do an in-depth investigation and spend the rest of the day trying to get me to move tables with my mind and read the teachers' thoughts. And I already knew *that* was a waste of time. I sighed again and shrugged.

"Well, I think that doctor sounds terrible," said Romy, rolling her eyes.

The bell rang just as I turned to open my locker and get my books for Mr. Martinez's class. All the other students had gone, and Romy and I were the only ones left in the hallway.

Romy saw it a fraction of a second before I realized what was happening. She raised her arm and pointed at my locker, her mouth hanging open from the shock. I turned my head and was immediately hit in the face by a shiny purple Doc Martens boot, the first in an avalanche of footwear spilling out of my locker and onto the floor.

"Ouch!" I yelled, falling back on my butt and lifting my arms to shield myself from the boots, and then the Converse in every possible color that rained down on top of me. Blurs of pink, sky blue, black polka dot, and candy-cane stripes flashed in front of me.

"What is going on?" I shouted.

Romy reached down and grabbed my outstretched hands, dodging a black patent Mary Jane that went whizzing by her head. We both stepped back, staring at the shoe mountain that continued to grow in front of my locker. I don't know much about physics—actually, I don't know anything about it; physics classes don't start until high school—but I just knew that the number of shoes pouring out of my locker defied the laws of nature. It wasn't possible for my four-foot-by-one-foot locker to hold what looked like the entire inventory of three shoe stores. Flip-flops, clogs, espadrilles, wedges, ballet slippers, tap shoes, high-tops, low-tops, soccer cleats, and even ice skates came spilling out.

"Where are they coming from?" whispered Romy. "How can there be so many?" She had the same awe-struck tone in her voice that Riley had had when he talked about the stars in the night sky during our camping trip to Maine last summer. Romy was still holding one of my hands, and I didn't let go.

My locker started to vibrate, and even though I realized it might explode and blast shards of metal at me and Romy, I could not move. I was both terrified and mesmerized by the torrent of shoes piling up in front of me.

Then the flow of shoes slowed to a trickle, like a spigot of water being turned off. For a fraction of a second there was nothing, and then a sparkly high-heeled shoe came flying out. It went sailing over the pile, hit the ground on the other side, and shattered into glass pieces.

"What kind of shoe was that?" asked Romy, letting go of my hand and bending down to examine the fragments. "What is going on?"

I moved slowly toward the tower of shoes and stood on tiptoe, peering over it into my open locker. My books were still on the shelf where I had left them the day before, my daily schedule was still pinned to the back of the locker, and my basketball shoes were still on the bottom shelf. Everything looked just as it had when I'd shut my locker yesterday.

"I don't know," I said. This was not a prank, for sure.

No kid at Hill Country Middle School (other than Romy, who was from one of the richest families in the state, though you'd never know it by the way she acted) had the ability or the resources to pull off something like this. And anyway, I wasn't popular enough to be the target of such an elaborate practical joke.

"Let's get rid of them," I said. "We can be late to math."

Making sure that we didn't have to explain the shoe tower in front of my locker to anyone was way more important than getting to class on time.

"We need to get rid of them!" I said again, but I couldn't move. I had an icky seasick feeling in the pit of my stomach as if the ground beneath me was moving. It felt like the world was turning upside down.

"I'm on it," said Romy. "Janitors' closet. I'll be right back." She took off running down the hallway.

She came back pushing a massive laundry basket—her head just visible over the top of it, as Romy is ballerina-tiny—that was usually used to collect athletic uniforms and lost-and-found items, and for the occasional joyride. Some sixth graders were still in detention for pulling that stunt last month.

I reached for the broom that Romy had stuck in the basket. I needed to do something to expel the anxious energy that was building inside me, so I started sweeping up the broken glass while Romy flung shoes into the laundry basket. She paused to admire a burgundy-colored ankle boot.

"These are cute," she said, waving it in front of me.

"Just take 'em, if you want," I said, trying not to look at the boot. I didn't want to catalog the bizarre contents of my locker. I didn't want to think about them. I just wanted to get rid of them as quickly as possible.

"Thanks, but I'm a six," she said, dropping the boot into the basket. "They're all eight and a half."

My size. They were all my size. I swallowed and let that piece of information sink in. Of course they were all my size. They were in my locker. A couple of weeks ago I would have been thrilled about being the beneficiary of a footwear bonanza—there were some really cute pairs of Converse in the pile—but looking at all these shoes made me feel sick. I had a nagging thought that their appearance was somehow related to me not sleeping. Not that they had anything in common, but finding hundreds of shoes crammed into your locker is weird. Not needing to sleep for eleven days is weird. And then there was the angry deer outside. The list of weird things that were happening to me just seemed to be getting longer. And weirder.

Once we had filled the laundry basket, Romy and I wheeled it back to the janitors' closet.

Romy took a piece of paper and a pen from a shelf and wrote a *Please Donate* note for the school janitor. I took the note from Romy and added, *There might be a dangerous deer in the parking lot* and then placed it on top of the shoe pile.

"What the . . . ?" said Romy, looking at what I'd written. "A dangerous deer?"

"Yeah." I sighed, pulling at my ripped T-shirt. "It attacked me on the way in. . . ."

"What?" gasped Romy.

"I'll tell you later," I said, starting to run down the hallway to retrieve my backpack. I just wanted to get to math class. Maybe algebra would take my mind off the strangest morning I had ever had.

Chapter 4

ALGEBRA DIDN'T WORK. NEITHER DID HISTORY or English. By the time Romy and I sat down for lunch, the *strange-things-are-happening* feeling I had experienced at the lockers had escalated into an all-out crisis occupying every bit of mental energy I had. I felt like my head was going to burst.

"Daadi made lunch," Romy said when I sat down. She slid a container of food toward me. She knew I loved her grandma's cooking.

"Yum," I said, scooping out the dal. There was no way I was eating the soup and bread roll I got from the

cafeteria counter when there was homemade Indian food on offer. "Will you ask her to make those sugary, milky ball things again?"

"Rasgullas," said Romy. "Yeah, sure." She bit into a roti. "Are you going to tell your dad about the shoes and the deer?"

"I dunno," I said.

I thought about the way Dad hadn't even considered the possibility that maybe I had actually stopped needing to sleep. What would he make of shoes spilling out of my locker and the deer's attempted assault? Dad wouldn't believe me. He'd tell me I must have imagined it, or he'd hint that I was exaggerating. I'd spent almost two weeks trying to convince him that I hadn't slept, and every time he'd said, *Ah, Cia, that's just not possible,* in his most reasonable voice, it had hurt. I didn't want to have any more of those conversations. I didn't want to give him more reasons to not believe me.

"No," I said. "I'm not going to tell him. There's no point."

"Okay," said Romy. She wiped her hands with a napkin, then put both elbows on the table. "So, you've stopped needing to sleep, you've been attacked by a deer, and hundreds of shoes have just appeared in your locker. . . ." She held up a hand, counting out the events on her fingers as she spoke.

I stared at the three fingers Romy had raised, feeling a sense of uneasiness. I'd been thinking exactly the same thing. Were the things happening to me connected? But how? What did sleep, an aggressive forest animal, and shoes have in common?

"How are these things connected?" continued Romy.

Romy looked determined, confused, and a little bit angry. It was the same look she got when she was doing her math homework.

"I don't know." I sighed. I leaned my elbows on the table and rested my chin on my hands. I glanced at the students at the tables around us, eating and chatting, probably talking about how soggy the cafeteria French fries were and whether or not Mr. Martinez had been wearing a new toupee in math class. I realized with a pang of disbelief that Romy and I were probably having the most interesting (and bizarre) conversation in the cafeteria. A horrible thought occurred to me: if these students knew about the morning I'd had, I'd be what they'd all be talking about. I felt my heart drop. It would be awful to be the number one gossip item in the whole school. I thought about Amy Petusky, a girl in my grade who had been fending off rumors that she was a werewolf. Amy had just had a really terrible unibrow. It was gone now—Mia Johnson had shown her how to wax it off—but jerks like Roger Wu still asked her how she was feeling when there was a full moon. Amy had just had some extra eyebrow hair, but I had a locker that defied the laws of nature and a condition that—according to my doctor—was physically impossible to have. What would everyone say about me? It would be brutal. I needed to stop that from ever happening. I had to figure out what was going on.

I glanced over at Romy. She had pulled out her phone and was tapping on it. "There's gotta be something," she muttered. "Let me just try . . . 'shoes and not sleeping' . . . 'shoes exploding in locker . . .'"

I knew from firsthand experience that Google was useless when you had questions that no one had ever asked before. I'd typed in *What happens when you don't need to sleep?* fifty different ways and had gotten about fifty thousand pointless search results.

I looked out again at the cafeteria. I couldn't believe it. John Lee was walking toward our table. This had to be the weirdest thing—amazing, yes, but also the weirdest thing—that had happened so far.

"Romy," I said, averting my eyes. "Don't look, but John Lee is walking right toward us."

My heart did the funny thump-skip-race thing it always did when I saw John Lee. Walking by tables and different groups, he ran a hand through his dark hair. He had really nice hair. When I'd mentioned this to Romy last week, she'd made a barf face. It wasn't that she didn't think John was cute—I was pretty sure every girl in our grade thought John was cute. Romy just thought the way I went on about him was ridiculous. But I couldn't help it.

Other than a weeklong infatuation with Archer Holmes in first grade (it had ended when I'd seen him pick up a half-eaten Jolly Rancher from underneath a slide and stick it in his mouth), I'd never "liked" a boy until John Lee moved here at the beginning of the school year. John

Lee had *dimples* when he smiled. And he played football—I didn't care much about sports, but apparently he was really good at it. Plus, he was smart. Rebecca Harrison, a girl in my science class, said she'd seen him reading *To Kill a Mockingbird*. For *fun*. It wasn't even assigned in a class. And he was nice. I'd seen him hold the door for Mrs. Talen when her arms were full of papers.

He was getting closer, and he was looking right at me. Was he actually going to sit at our table? My heart hammered so hard I felt winded, like I'd just done twenty push-ups. I felt my cheeks getting warmer and knew that my face was becoming a big blushing blob of embarrassment. I might as well have held up a sign and waved it in front of John as he approached: *I like you. I think you're the cutest guy in the grade.*

"Cia," Romy whispered, looking pointedly at my red cheeks. "Just relax."

Just relax? Relax? How could I relax? This was the moment I'd been dreaming about. I only had one class with John, and I'd never managed to have a conversation with him. Now it was about to happen. I was going to talk to him. What was I wearing? A ripped T-shirt. Ugh. Why hadn't I gotten any hoop earrings? I'd read somewhere that they projected confidence and positive energy. What would I say to him? My mouth had gone completely dry. I felt like my lips were glued together. He was almost at the table. My lungs tightened in my chest.

"Just breathe," muttered Romy. What was she talking about? Did I look like I was hyperventilating? Was I going to pass out? Maybe I should pass out. I could just sort of fall into his arms. . . .

"Hey."

John was speaking to me. He had stopped and was standing beside Romy on the other side of the table. I stared at him for a fraction of a second and then dropped my eyes down. I couldn't look at him.

"Hey," I squeaked.

"You dropped this," he said, putting a pink velvet scrunchie on the table. I recognized it. I'd used it to put my hair in a low ponytail this morning. I hadn't realized it had fallen out.

"Thanks," I mumbled, looking up, but John had already turned around and started walking away. I stared at the scrunchie.

"He brought me my scrunchie," I gasped, pointing at the hair tie in the middle of the table.

"Yeah," said Romy, taking a forkful of her food. "So, I didn't find anything on Google. . . ."

"Romy, John Lee brought me my scrunchie," I repeated. How could she even think about eating? This was huge. John had walked across the cafeteria to bring me my scrunchie. It was like . . .

"Didn't knights bring ladies their handkerchiefs when they dropped them as, like, symbols of, you know . . ." I paused. If I said "love," Romy might throw a bread roll at me. "Their esteem?"

Romy stared at me blankly.

"Symbols of their esteem?" She raised an eyebrow. "Cia, he just brought you a hair tie. It's not like he had to fight a dragon to get over here."

"When do you think he picked it up?" I asked, reaching up to touch my hair. I was pretty sure I still had it in a ponytail in history class. Maybe he saw it fall out when I was going to English. That would mean he'd held on to it for at least an hour. My scrunchie had been in John Lee's possession for an hour.

My heart started racing again. I reached over, picked it up, and held it carefully in the palm of my hand.

"How long do you think he had it?" I asked Romy as I gazed down at my scrunchie.

"Gimme that," said Romy, grabbing the scrunchie out of my hand. She put it on her wrist. "You can have this back when you calm down." She leaned forward in her chair. "Now, are we going to talk about John's quest to reunite you with your scrunchie, or all the other stuff that's been going on?"

I sighed. "All the other stuff that's been going on." I really did want to keep talking about John and how amazing it was that he had brought me my scrunchie, but Romy wasn't going to stand for it—which was, I thought, a bit unfair, seeing as how I'd had to spend hours almost every day last summer listening to her going on about a hot lifeguard from her trip to the beach.

"Right," said Romy, getting back to business. "Has anything else happened to you? Anything else that's weird?"

"Hmm," I said, casting a quick glance around the cafeteria to see if John was looking in my direction. But I couldn't see him anywhere.

"Cia!" snapped Romy. "Has anything else happened?"

"Sorry," I said. "Yeah, there is something else." I realized that I hadn't told Romy about what Dad had said after we'd gone to Dr. Loomis's. "Apparently, Mom took me to a baby-whisperer—baby *sleep*-whisperer—when I was, you know, a baby because I couldn't sleep. And it worked."

"So, this has happened before, you not needing to sleep?" gasped Romy, eyes widening.

"I dunno," I said, suddenly feeling defensive, as if Romy had just accused me of doing something wrong. "I mean, lots of babies don't sleep. It's not weird for a baby to not sleep. . . ." But I wasn't absolutely sure about that. I hadn't been around a lot of babies.

"Yeah, but going to a baby sleep-whisperer," said Romy, dropping her voice. "That's kinda weird, Cia."

It was. We both sat in silence for a moment.

Romy slammed a hand down on the table. "I've got it," she said. "I bet this sleep-whisperer can help you. They'll make you fall asleep now, Cia. They did it before!"

"Umm . . ." I didn't love that idea. I sort of agreed with Dad that sleep-whispering sounded like a lot of hocus-pocus, and I didn't want to be hocus-pocused or whatever it was that a sleep-whisperer did.

But I'd tried a doctor. And that had been no help. Not only did Dr. Loomis not know anything, but she hadn't even believed me. So maybe a sleep-whisperer was exactly the sort of expert I needed.

"Okay," I said. "I guess I could try a sleep-whisperer. . . ."

"Great! How do we get in touch with them?"

"I don't know," I said, my heart dropping. So much for that idea. "I don't know where they are. Or who they are. I don't even know if they're still in business."

"What about your mom? Just ask her," offered Romy. "She's the one who took you."

"She's not back until Friday night."

"Friday? You can't wait that long," said Romy, eyes widening, biting her lip. She didn't say it, but I knew what she was thinking. The way things were going, anything could happen in three days.

"I'll text her," I said, even though I knew Mom had no cell reception. I felt like I still had to try.

As soon as I pressed send, an error message popped up. *Undeliverable.*

I groaned and threw my phone down on the table. It skidded toward Romy.

"Are you still mad at her?" asked Romy, gently sliding my phone back.

I shrugged. I'd told Romy about the fight I'd had with Mom the night before she left on her trip.

"Not really. Maybe."

"She just tried to give you a present," said Romy.

"It's not about that." I sighed. But I knew it wasn't Romy's fault that she didn't understand. Her mom wasn't like mine. Her mom just wanted Romy to get good grades and play the cello and a couple of sports. My mom acted like she expected me to win a Nobel Prize before I graduated high school. I felt like nothing I did was ever good enough for her.

"Okay, okay. What about your dad? Would he know anything about this baby-whisperer?" said Romy, changing the subject.

"Nah." I shook my head. Dad couldn't even remember what electives I was taking this year (PE and choir); there was no way he'd remember details about an almost-thirteen-year-old appointment that Mom had probably just told him about. Mom was the one who kept track of my and Riley's activities. Something occurred to me. "I could check in the attic. There's a bunch of boxes with my name on them. . . ." I'd noticed them last time I was up there, when I helped Dad put away the Christmas decorations. My name had been written on them in Mom's handwriting. "I can take a look to see if there's—"

"Any clues," said Romy, going into full investigative mode.

"Yeah," I said, glancing at the clock on the cafeteria wall. There was still two more hours before school finished, and then I could search our attic. It felt good to have a plan. Well, a bit of a plan.

"You coming to the auditions later?" asked Romy.

I had thought about trying out for the role of the nurse because whoever played her got to wear a wacky medieval headpiece and run around the stage interrupting Juliet and saying the wrong thing all the time. The nurse was the one who made the audience laugh.

But I found myself saying, "I'm going to skip it."

Last year I'd made the sixth grade basketball team, and Mom came to every game and whooped and hollered so much that the coach had to tell her to quiet down. It had been mortifying. I'd just wanted to be part of a team, but Mom had acted like I was on my way to the WNBA. She'd even given me a book titled *Women in Sports: 50 Fearless Athletes Who Played to Win.* (I had added it to the bottom of my shelf with other books Mom gave me that I didn't want, like *Six Exceptional Kids Who Are Changing the World* and a *Be Fearless* coloring book.) Once, when I mentioned that being an attorney sounded like a cool job, she went out and bought a black robe and a gavel so that I could "practice being a Supreme Court justice." If I ever expressed the tiniest bit of interest in anything, Mom would go into over-the-top motivational mode, and I'd forget why I'd wanted to do it in the first place. If I were in a school play, she'd think I was destined to be a Broadway star, and she'd sign me up for workshops with a voice coach and a dance instructor.

"But the play'll be awesome! It'll be so much fun," argued Romy.

But it wouldn't be for me. Not with my mom.

"It's just not my thing." I pushed back my chair and got up.

Romy knew I wasn't telling the truth. At our last sleepover we'd rehearsed a scene between Juliet and the nurse. I'd even tied a pillow to my head to get into character.

"I gotta get to social studies," I said. I put my hand out. "Can I have my scrunchie back?"

Romy pulled it off her wrist and gave it to me.

She grinned. "Are you going to frame it?"

Chapter 5

SCIENCE, MY LAST CLASS OF THE DAY, WAS THE one and only class I had with John Lee. For a few brief, awesome moments last month, we had been lab partners before Mrs. Taylor decided that Gavin Shortt and Vikram Rawie needed to be split up after Gavin singed Vikram's eyebrows with a Bunsen burner before class had even started. So, I ended up with Gavin "Fire-Starter" Shortt and lost my chance to have an actual conversation with John.

I spent most of social studies—the class I had before science—replaying what had happened in the cafeteria, gradually realizing, the more I thought about it, that I had acted like such a dork in front of John. Why hadn't I said something interesting or funny? All I'd done was turn red and squeak at him. Maybe I should have acted super casual instead of gaping like my brain had stopped working. No wonder he'd just dropped the scrunchie and practically run away from my fire-engine red face. I'd had a chance to have a conversation with John Lee, to show him how nice and cool I was (well, nice, anyway—maybe not cool), and I'd blown it. What was I going to do now? Start dropping pencils and erasers in his path, hoping that he'd pick them up and run after me?

I kept my head down in class, forcing myself not to look at the back of John's head—which was what I sometimes did when the class got boring—counting the moments until the bell rang and I could go home and search the attic. But then Gavin Shortt flung his notebook on the ground—he claimed he was trying to get rid of a fly—and John turned around and smiled. Right at me. My heart jumped as I considered the possibility that maybe I hadn't blown my chance after all.

I held on to that thought as I walked home and

wondered if the dropping-pencils idea wasn't really such a bad strategy (though I could just imagine Romy rolling her eyes if I told her about it). When I reached our front door, I braced myself for what I knew was waiting for me on the other side: Riley and his Nerf blaster. He'd gotten it for his sixth birthday a few months ago and had ambushed me every day since. I opened the door just a fraction and peered in. No sign of him. He usually attacked from the stairs. Maybe he'd found a new cat video to watch and forgotten the time. I smiled, thinking about how much he'd laugh if I snuck upstairs to his room, grabbed his blaster, and attacked him for a change.

I stepped inside, and—*boom*—a barrage of foam darts rained down on me. He'd just been biding his time. Riley scrambled off a kitchen stool that he must have dragged into the hallway and took off running. I flung my back-pack onto the ground and charged after him, grabbing him as he rounded a corner into the living room, and we both fell onto the sofa.

"Gimme that," I gasped, reaching for the blaster.

"I got you!" shouted Riley, jumping up and down.

"You got me," I croaked, sprawling out on the sofa as

if I'd been fatally injured. I grabbed the blaster and threw it on the floor. "How about a hug?" I asked, sitting back up. "How was school?"

"Good," he said, wriggling out of my arms. "I've got something for you."

He ran over to the kitchen counter and came back with a piece of paper. He handed it to me. It was a picture of two stick figures holding hands. The smaller one had an *R* on its T-shirt—obviously, this one was Riley—and the bigger one had loads of scribbled hair and was wearing a huge medal.

"Is this supposed to me?" I asked, pointing at it.

"Yeah."

"Why do I have a medal?"

"'Cause you're the best sister in the world."

I was surprised to feel my chest getting tight. I knew little kids said "best" all the time, like it was no big deal—every other video Riley watched and ice cream he tasted was "the best"—but it still felt really nice to hear him use it to describe me. I wasn't actually the best at anything. Not a sport or a musical instrument or math or a language or anything. But maybe I was a pretty good sister. I let Riley blast me with his Nerf gun every day and had read *The Big Book of Outrageous Facts* to him so many times that I practically knew it all by heart.

"Ah, Riley," I said. "Thanks. C'mon, you need a medal too."

I got up, grabbed a pencil from a kitchen drawer, and put Riley's picture on the counter. He scrambled up onto a stool beside me.

"You do it, Cia."

Dad walked into the kitchen as I was drawing the medal onto the Riley stick figure.

"Hey, Cia," he said, reaching by me to get an apple from the fruit bowl. "Anything interesting happen at school?"

"Nope," I lied.

"C'mon, Riley, I gotta get you to practice," said Dad. "I'm just gonna get changed. Be back in five minutes."

Riley sank down onto the stool. "I don't wanna go."

"But you love soccer, Ri," I said. He was always dribbling his soccer ball around the chairs in the dining room and using the fireplace as a goal. "What's going on?"

"I'm not good at it." He frowned, holding back tears. "Everyone else is faster and better than me."

"That's not true!" I'd been to a few of Riley's games. Most of the kids never even made contact with the ball, and a couple of them spent the entire time tying their shoelaces.

"Hayes Morgan said I'm no good at it."

"Hayes Morgan!" I sputtered. I'd never heard the name before, but I guessed he was a kid in Riley's class. "Is he a famous soccer player?"

Riley shook his head.

"Then he's gotta be a professional sports commentator?"

Riley shook his head again, and I saw the smallest hint of a smile.

"Then why are you listening to him? Hayes Morgan doesn't know what he's talking about. You love soccer. Don't stop doing what you love just because a boy in your class said something stupid."

"Will you come watch me?" he asked, his face brightening a little. "I'll go if you come."

"Ri, I—" I thought about all the boxes in the attic I needed to search and how I might finally be able to find answers to the questions that had been worrying me all day. But I couldn't stand it when Riley was sad.

"'Course I'll come with you."

Soccer practice wrapped up in less than an hour, and then Dad and Riley dropped me off at home and headed out for pizza. As soon as they pulled away, I raced up to the attic and found about thirty boxes with my name on them. I wished Romy was with me. This was a two-person job. I sent her a text to check on how the audition was going.

Then I got started.

The first box I checked had been mislabeled. It said CIA on the outside, but inside there was just a bunch of newspaper clippings, articles, and books that Mom must have read when she was getting her PhD. All about fairy tales. Mom couldn't get enough of that stuff. She had a stack of books on her bedside table, all of them about fairy tales from all over the world. I'd wandered into my parents' bedroom a few nights ago looking for something to read and had started a story called "The Girl without Hands," a Brothers Grimm tale. It was creepy. If I'd still been sleeping, it would have given me nightmares.

The next box had the usual standard baby keepsakes inside it: the tiny ID bracelet I wore in the hospital and cute booties. So far, so normal. But at the bottom I found my used, chewed-up pacifiers, baby bottles, and even a bag of my toenail clippings, which was just gross. Why on earth had Mom wanted to save that stuff? In the third box I checked, I found a journal entitled *Cia* containing pages and pages of Mom's writing detailing everything from my first steps to my first day of kindergarten. My heart started hammering in my chest as I read her descriptions of five-year-old me.

Cia is brave. Cia is not afraid of anything. Cia will find her path and overcome any obstacles. Cia knows what she wants.

Was this true? Had I been a fearless five-year-old? Other than the standoff with Mom over the Belle dress—which I had *lost*—I didn't remember much about being five. When did Mom stop believing that I could overcome any obstacles? *Why* did she stop believing that? I thought about the journal she'd given me on my last birthday. It was called *Do One Thing Every Day That Scares You*. I hated that gift. I'd never thought of myself as being a frightened kid, but when Mom gave me a journal with, as the back cover said, "a year's worth of fear-facing prompts," I had started to wonder. Maybe I was a scaredy-cat.

Maybe I wasn't brave.

I read some more.

Cia read the word "cat" today. I'm so proud of her!

Cia fell off her bike and got right back on. What a girl!

I felt a lump in my throat. Why couldn't Mom be happy like this now, with me just doing normal stuff? Just being a seventh grader who got good—not brilliant, but still good—grades and was, according to Riley anyway, the best sister in the world.

I couldn't get rid of the lump in my throat, and now my eyes were starting to sting. I thought about the terrible "surprise" she had put in my room the night before she had left on her trip. When I'd gotten home from school, I'd gone upstairs to my room to do homework and found it on my wall. It was an enormous canvas poster that stretched from the floor to the ceiling and spelled out, in capital letters that were as tall as me, the words: DREAM BIG AND WRITE YOUR OWN STORY. It was framed with tiny lights that flashed on and off, making it look like a billboard in Times Square.

When I yelled out "MOM!" and she came running into my room, I told her that I hated it and was taking it down, and she argued that I needed to be reminded that I could write my own story. She said that she wanted me to know that I could do anything. I still pulled it off the wall and told her to take it away. But I hadn't told her why it had upset me so much. I hadn't really known myself. But now, sitting in the attic surrounded by the evidence of how proud Mom had once been of me, I understood. When Mom told me to "dream big" and "write my own story," it made me feel like she believed that I wasn't dreaming big enough, that I wasn't already writing my own story. When she left a note in my back-pack telling me to "shine," it made me feel like I wasn't shining bright enough. Like I wasn't enough. I wasn't talented enough, or brave enough, to be the daughter she wanted.

I brushed a tear away, wondering if I'd find more journals that showed how proud Mom had once been of me. Then my fingers touched a single sheet of paper. I lifted it out and looked at it. This was it. I wiped my eyes.

This was what I had come to the attic hoping to find.

The paper had a border of line-drawn cherub babies along the edge, each one smiling and looking adorable (and also maybe a little creepy). There were three verses on the page, and the first one had been circled in red pen.

I read it.

Is getting your baby to sleep a terrible chore?
With Madame Fredepia you will fret no more.
Replace crying and colic with giggles and calm.
Restore peace to your home with her patented charm.

This had to be the person Mom had taken me to.

What will life bring to your bundle of joy?
Come learn the answer, be it a girl or a boy.
And if the Fates show sorrow and hardship will come,
With Madame Fredepia such a future's undone.

Okay, that bit sounded more witchy woman than Mary Poppins.

I read the third and final verse.

Whatever future you choose for your precious child,
Madame Fredepia can deliver once the debt's
reconciled.
Madame Fredepia has gifts to bestow.
Open Monday through Friday with coffee to go.

"Debt's reconciled," I mumbled. That seemed creepy. And I didn't like the line with "if the Fates show sorrow and hardship will come," either. I turned the page over. The other side was blank.

I grabbed my phone and typed *Madame Fredepia* into Google. I noticed my hand was shaking and that the attic seemed stiflingly hot all of a sudden. There was one search result.

Madame Fredepia, Fortune-Teller

Just those four words followed by an address. I almost dropped my phone from the shock when I read it. The address was Grafton Market, Brooklyn, New York.

Grafton Market was the name of the small cluster of shops that were within walking distance of my school. There was a frozen yogurt shop, Yo-Yo Swirl, where Romy and I and about half of my middle school hung out all the time. I'd never seen any sign of a fortune-telling shop or whatever you call it, and it seemed like that was something you would notice. How was it possible that Madame Fredepia had been working there and I had never noticed?

I stuck the paper in my back pocket and texted Romy.

It was only 5:30 p.m. Madame Fredepia might still be open for business.

Meet me at Yo-Yo Swirl. I've found the baby-whisperer.

Romy was locking her bike at the stand outside Yo-Yo Swirl when I arrived.

"How'd the audition go?" I asked, coming alongside her.

"Pretty great." She grinned. She took the paper I'd found in the attic from my hand and started reading it.

"That's awesome," I said. I took off my helmet and attached it to my bike, glancing through the big window of the yogurt shop. I saw a group of students in our grade standing by the order counter.

"This is cool . . . ," said Romy, handing me back the paper. "What does 'such a future's undone' mean?"

I shrugged and put the paper in my pocket. *Was* it cool? I'd just thought it was kind of creepy. I looked through the window of Yo-Yo Swirl again. I wished that that was what Romy and I were doing, just hanging out having frozen yogurt like a couple of normal middle schoolers, not tracking down someone named Madame Fredepia.

"Maybe she can tell me if I'll get the part of Juliet," said Romy, brightening.

"I think she might just specialize in babies. . . ."

"But still, a fortune-teller . . . ," said Romy excitedly. "I've always wanted to go to a fortune-teller."

Romy was so fired up that she started bouncing on the balls of her feet like she was about to ride a roller coaster. I felt glad that she was with me. Romy was so excited, I could almost pretend that this was something fun and not a desperate effort to find out why strange things were happening to me.

"Let's do this," I said. I followed Romy's gaze as she looked at each storefront.

Grafton Market is small. From our position outside the yogurt shop, we could see all six of the other businesses: a dry cleaner's, pet supplies store, nail salon, clothes boutique, and sandwich shop. No fortune-teller.

Then a chewed-up tennis ball—maybe a castaway

from the pet store—rolled along the sidewalk that we were standing on and proceeded down the alleyway beside the yogurt shop. I watched its progress until it stopped in front of a door. A door I'd never seen before, or maybe I had just never looked closely down that alleyway before.

Romy and I walked toward it. We both paused to look at the lettering on the front.

MADAME FREDEPIA

FORTUNES TOLD

PSYCHIC GUIDES FOUND

MAGIC DISPENSED

And then in print so tiny I had to squint to read it:

ALL CONSULTATIONS ARE FINAL. FULL PAYMENT MUST BE MADE AT TIME OF SERVICE. MADAME FREDEPIA DOES NOT GUARANTEE, WARRANT, OR VOUCH FOR ANY GOODS OR SERVICES.

And then in even tinier print:

MADAME FREDEPIA IS A LICENSED MEMBER OF THE LFGM.

I didn't know what the LFGM was. I made a mental note to look it up later.

"Magic dispensed," said Romy, sounding impressed.

"The *a* is missing, and the *d* is about to fall off," I

~ 67 ~

said. I pointed at the wonky lettering on the door.

Romy stood back and motioned at the door, like a porter at a fancy hotel welcoming a guest.

"Shall we?" she said.

"We shall." I reached for the door.

Chapter 6

I TURNED THE HANDLE AND STEPPED INTO A living room. The first thing I noticed was the smell of smoke—either candle or cigarette, I wasn't sure. The second thing I noticed were the books. Every surface in the room—the upholstered armchairs, the tables, and even the mud-colored rug on the floor—was covered with books stacked haphazardly on top of one another. The books looked old, possibly should-be-in-a-museum old. Nearly all of them were bound in leather and had gold lettering along the spines and on the covers. For a moment I forgot why I was there, and my hands itched to pick up one of them and look through it.

"Hello!" shouted Romy into the empty room.

There was a rustle of fabric, and a woman stepped out from behind a curtain. She was about my mother's age, and she was dressed in typical mom clothes. Jeans, cardigan, sneakers. She looked like she'd be more at home getting her nails done at the place next door than in this out-of-time library/living room.

"Madame Fredepia?" I asked.

"Amazing," said the woman breathlessly, coming so close to me that I could see that her eyes were blazing with excitement and her mascara was smudged. "Madame Fredepia is amazing. She has connected me to my spirit guide. A vizier at the court of Cleopatra. He told me that I am destined for great things."

She pushed her shoulders back in a determined manner, opened the front door, and walked out, trailing the dry-cleaning she must have picked up before her session with the vizier behind her.

I looked at Romy, and she gave me the raised eyebrows, *that-was-wild* expression. I grimaced and nodded in agreement.

I walked over to the curtain and pulled it back a couple of inches.

"Madame Fredepia?" I said to the tall Black woman who was standing beside a large round table that took up most of the space in the alcove. The table was covered with a red, velvety-fringed cloth, and on it was a crystal ball, glowing white like a massive light bulb, and a deck of tarot cards with the grim reaper and the queen faceup.

The woman pulled a scarf off her head and flung it on the table, its metallic coins clinking when they hit the surface. She had curly black hair that was streaked with silver, but she had no wrinkles on her face.

I'd never visited a fortune-teller, but I knew what fortune-tellers were supposed to dress like. They were supposed to dress like the woman in front of me. She was covered in a confection of silver, velvet, lace, and jangly jewelry. Her skirt looked like something you'd find in a costume store—it was so voluminous, Romy and I both could have hidden underneath it. She had rings on every finger, charm bracelets on both wrists, and pendants hanging around her neck, some of them disappearing into the folds of her ruffly white blouse.

"I'm closed," she said, without looking over at me. "That Cleopatra business wore me out."

"Please. It'll only take a minute," I said, stepping into the alcove to show her that I was serious. She had to hear me out. She'd contacted ancient Egypt for the woman before us; I only had one question. "I just need to ask you about something."

"Well, I'm not answering," she said, still not looking at me. "I'm closed. It's been a long day. My feet are killing me."

She sat down on the chair beside the table, stretching out her legs, and a pair of shiny high-heeled shoes peeked out from under her skirt. They looked much too dainty for anyone other than a ballerina. No wonder her feet were sore.

She reached across the table and grabbed a white statue of a blindfolded, toga-wearing woman. I recognized it as a statue of Fortuna, the Roman goddess of luck. Turning the head of the woman, Madame Fredepia lifted it right off and placed it on the table. She stuck her hand in what was left of the statue and pulled out a cigarette and lighter. She put the cigarette in her mouth and lit it, took a long drag, and then from behind a haze of smoke she looked back and forth from me to Romy. Then she smiled, and her face became lovely, her cheeks rounded out like two red apples, and her eyes seemed to twinkle.

"Oh," she said, pointing her cigarette at me. "I've seen you before. You have the mark."

Chapter 7

"THE WHAT?" SAID ROMY, LOOKING BACK AND forth between me and Madame Fredepia.

"You have the mark," Madame Fredepia repeated, nodding her head at me. "There's a shimmer of yellow all around you. Definitely my work. My work always comes out yellow."

Romy stared at me. "I can't see anything."

"You don't have the sight," sniffed Madame Fredepia. "You wouldn't be able to see an aura if it were glowing like a Christmas tree." She narrowed her eyes at Romy and added, "You're a good friend, though."

I held out my arms in front of me and examined them, terrified that I'd see a radioactive haze wafting off me. But I couldn't see anything. I felt myself relax, and I pushed away the thought that maybe, like Romy, I didn't have "the sight" and that was why I wasn't seeing anything.

"So, you have seen me before?" I asked, wanting to make sure I understood correctly what Madame Fredepia was saying. "You saw me when I was a baby?"

I pulled out the piece of paper from my back pocket and handed it to her. She took it from me, glanced at it, and placed it on the table.

"That was a long time ago," she said almost wistfully. "I only do the occasional baby now. Far too unpredictable." She paused and leaned forward. "No matter how excellent a spell caster is—and I can assure you I am one of the best—using magic on babies is a very messy business." She shook her head and put her palms up. "Oh no, I'll only do a baby now if the circumstances are dire."

"But you"—I said, wondering about what dire circumstances a baby might get themselves into—"did me?"

"Looks like it," said Madame Fredepia, kicking off her shoes and revealing stripy red-and-white socks.

"I think my mom took me to see you because I couldn't sleep . . . and then after she took me . . . I slept."

"Nice to know she got value for money. Have you come back to thank me?"

"Well, no," I said, but I wondered if I should thank Madame Fredepia. Would that make her more likely to tell me about what had happened? "I mean . . . thank you. . . . The thing is, I did go to sleep *then*, but now I can't sleep—I mean at *all*—and I wondered if the two things might be connected . . . me not needing to sleep anymore . . ."

Madame Fredepia sat up straighter in her chair and stared at me for so long, I wondered if she had gone into some fortune-teller-type trance.

"How long has it been?" she finally said. "Since you slept."

"Eleven days."

She mouthed the words "eleven days" and then stared at me as if looking at me for the first time.

"And your hair?" she asked, pointing at my head. "How is your hair?"

My hair. What did my hair have to do with anything?

I glanced over at Romy. She leaned over and inspected the back of my head.

"Your hair looks fine," she said, sounding confused. "Like it always does."

"Why are you asking me about my hair?" I asked Madame Fredepia.

"Because—" said Madame Fredepia excitedly, but then she stopped as if she had changed her mind about something. She got up from her chair. "You know, I'm going to get into something a bit more comfortable. . . . You don't mind if I get out of this, do you?" She pointed at her skirt and ruffly blouse. "A lot of people expect the full costume, and white people seem to love this nonsense." She winked at Romy, who let out a snort of laughter. Just yesterday, Romy told Mia Johnson to stop giving her fashion tips when Mia had told her that she should wear saris all the time.

I didn't care what Madame Fredepia wore—she could change into her pajamas for all I cared—just as long as she told me about what was going on.

"Go and sit back in there," said Madame Fredepia, pointing to the living room we had just walked through.

"Find a comfy seat. I'll be right with you."

Romy and I returned to the living room, and Romy selected a worn-out-looking brown velvet sofa that, judging by the way it sagged when she sat on it, was older than my grandparents. There was a *People* magazine on the table beside the sofa. Romy picked it up and started leafing through it. I couldn't sit down. I felt too twitchy and nervous. What was Madame Fredepia going to tell me? When I'd mentioned the not-sleeping thing, she had snapped to attention and stared at me like I was some fascinating specimen under a microscope. And then there was her mysterious comment about my hair—not to mention what she'd said about me having a yellow mark. What was all that about?

Within a moment or two Madame Fredepia came into the living room wearing a rosy pink turtleneck, tailored cream pants, and suede beige pumps. If this was what she meant by "comfortable," I couldn't imagine what her formal wear was like. Her nails, which had been painted a fire-engine red when we came in, were now a pale blue. How had she managed to get changed and give herself a manicure in less than a minute?

"This is better," she said, sitting down on an armchair next to the sofa. "Feel more like myself now." She looked at me. "You need to sit down. I'm going to strain my neck looking up at you."

I sat down on the sofa beside Romy.

Madame Fredepia pointed at the magazine Romy was holding. There was a good-looking, smiley couple on the cover with the words $100 MILLION DIVORCE printed underneath them. "Some people just can't hold on to their happily ever after."

She sighed sadly.

"So, Cia." She turned to me.

Had I told her my name? No, I hadn't. Did Madame Fredepia just remember the names of everyone she'd ever seen or was there something magicky going on?

"You're not sleeping, but your hair is fine." I felt a pang of anxiety. Why was she bringing up hair again? "Now, what else has happened that you'd call *unusual*?" She emphasized the last word, so it came out as *un-YOU-shew-al*.

I started with the shoes in my locker, and before I'd even gotten to the possibly rabid deer and my sighting of the winged figure in our backyard, Madame Fredepia clapped her hands excitedly.

"Ah, the shoes and the not sleeping!" she said, nodding and smiling as if she'd just figured out the answer to a really hard crossword puzzle. She added, almost to herself, "Of course those two things would go together."

"But, what?" I asked, working hard to keep my voice steady. "What do shoes have to do with me not sleeping?" I glanced over at Romy. She was staring at Madame Fredepia, her mouth hanging open ever so slightly, like she needed more oxygen than usual. I looked back at Madame Fredepia. I didn't like the expression on her face. She looked delighted, like a kid unwrapping their birthday presents. Why was she so excited?

"Well, one is Cinderella, and the other is Sleeping Beauty," said Madame Fredepia in the same down-to-earth way as if we were talking about the weather or restaurants. "Cinderella lost her shoe, so now a *lot* of shoes have, well, found you. And Sleeping Beauty slept for an awfully long time, and you don't need to sleep at all." She beamed at me as if that settled everything.

"Why? What? Huh?" asked Romy, sounding stunned

and looking back and forth between me and Madame Fredepia. "Why are you talking about fairy tales?"

"Because," said Madame Fredepia in a tone that made it sound like she couldn't believe Romy was asking such a ludicrous question, "what's happening to Cia is simply the opposite of what happened in those particular fairy tales."

I stared at Madame Fredepia. I knew fortune-tellers were supposed to say wacky things, but this? This was just silly! Why would I be doing the opposite of what happened in fairy tales?

But even as I told myself that Madame Fredepia was talking nonsense, I felt a horrible, icky feeling building inside me and sweat pooling under my armpits. What she was saying was incredibly weird, but very weird things were happening to me, and wouldn't it make sense that the explanation for those things would be incredibly weird?

I let out a little groan. Romy put her hand on my arm as if to steady me.

"But why?" said Romy, whipping her head back and forth between me and Madame Fredepia. "Why would Cia do the opposite of what happened in fairy tales?"

"It's because of the spell," said Madame Fredepia. She reached into a bowl of what looked like marbles on the small table beside her.

"The spell?" I gasped.

"Yes, the spell," repeated Madame Fredepia, putting one of the marble candies in her mouth. "The one I put on you."

Chapter 8

I COULDN'T SPEAK. I COULDN'T THINK. I JUST SAT there with my mouth open, gasping for air. I had been spelled. I felt a wave of nausea hit me, and I collapsed onto the sofa. The downward slide was so acute that my knees almost hit my chin and I ended up with my bottom wedged into the back of the sofa, with my legs sticking out in front of me.

Romy was able to speak first. "You put a spell on Cia?" she said, managing to sound both shocked and furious at the same time.

"What?" I said, pushing myself up from the crack I

was wedged into. "What are you talking about?" It took an enormous effort just to get the words out; my heart was racing so fast.

Mom. It was all her fault. She took me to this woman and let her put a spell on me. What was wrong with my mom? Other moms didn't go around taking their babies to fortune-tellers and asking them to use *spells* to make them go to sleep. The anger must have shown on my face because Madame Fredepia pulled her chair even closer to the sofa and spoke to me firmly.

"Now, don't be blaming your mother. She didn't even know about the second spell."

The second spell? How many spells were there?

"She was in such a terrible state when she came to me. Poor thing hadn't gotten a full night's sleep for weeks and weeks. She was exhausted. Had no idea how hard having a baby was going to be. She just wanted some help getting you to sleep. And I'd found a nice little spell that made babies sleep through the night. Put a bit of powdered newt's tail and aniseed into your bottle. Nothing to it, really."

She reached into the container of marble candies,

pulled out a cigarette, and pinched the tip with her fingers, and it lit up. Then she put it in her mouth and inhaled. I exchanged a glance with Romy. Was that actual magic? Or some new self-lighting brand of cigarette?

"So, that was that. But then your mother . . . Well, she just kept talking. She told me that she wanted you to be a strong woman . . . to be self-reliant. She didn't want you to grow up and buy into any of that princess, one-day-my-prince-will-come-and-make-my-life-wonderful nonsense."

That sounded like my mom, all right.

"Well, I did think she was being a bit unfair. . . . Those princesses are just looking for their happily ever afters, aren't they? Nothing wrong with that."

She paused and looked at me expectantly. I nodded even though I wasn't sure what I was agreeing to. I just wanted her to keep explaining.

"So, your mother said that she'd love to make you"—she pointed a finger at me—"'immune to the charms of fairy tales.' And I thought, why not? Definitely a challenge, but I could give it a go. No harm in throwing in a freebie every now and again. Didn't even tell your mom I did it." She winked at me. "You know mothers and daughters.

Can be such a tricky relationship—lots of love, but lots of expectations . . ." She looked at me knowingly.

Had Mom had absurd expectations for me when I was a baby? No, she hadn't. I thought about what I'd read in her journal in the attic. Did Madame Fredepia know that Mom had impossible expectations for me now?

"But what did you *do*?" asked Romy impatiently.

"A counterspell."

"A counterspell?" I sputtered.

"That's the one," said Madame Fredepia delightedly. "And I didn't even know it worked until you came in here today." She sat back in her chair, beamed at me and Romy, and then sighed happily as if she couldn't quite believe how fantastically well everything was going. I felt like shouting at her, but Romy got there first.

"But what does it do?" she demanded. "What does the spell do?"

"It's a spell that makes things run counter. An opposing spell," said Madame Fredepia, circling her hands in opposite directions. "And a very tricky one. Lot of talent needed to administer a counterspell." She paused and gave me a significant look.

I glared back at her. Was she expecting me to be impressed? Did she think I was going to congratulate her? Or thank her? She didn't seem at all upset by my reaction and kept on going in the same gushy way. "I did a spell that would make absolutely sure that you"—she paused and looked at me—"would never be influenced by 'all that princess nonsense,' as your mother called it. And there are a lot of princesses." She paused and breathed out dramatically as if she were still recovering from the effort of casting the spell. "Well, the energies get pushed back with a counterspell. It means that whatever happened to the girls in the fairy tales, the opposite, the contrary, will happen to you." She paused again and got a faraway look in her eyes. "Interesting that it ended up being so literal . . . That's a surprise. . . ."

"Cinderella lost a shoe . . . ," said Romy.

"And all those shoes turned up in my locker," I said, the meaning of Madame Fredepia's words beginning to sink in.

"Yeah." Romy nodded. "Shoes *literally* showed up in your locker. The reverse of what happened to Cinderella . . ."

"But hang on . . . Cinderella losing the shoe isn't the most important part of that story," I said.

Madame Fredepia shrugged her shoulders. "Don't look at me. I didn't write the counterspell. I just cast it."

"But if the prince hadn't found the shoe, he never would have found Cinderella, and they wouldn't have, you know, lived happily ever after," added Romy. "So maybe it is the most important part."

My mind raced, sorting through all the other fairy tales I knew.

"Snow White?" I asked. "What about her?"

"You'll live with seven giants and never eat apples?" said Romy. She spoke so fast, she was a little breathless. Maybe I would have been excited to find out magic was real too if this were happening to her and not me. But this wasn't fun; it was terrifying.

"'Rapunzel'? 'Beauty and the Beast' . . . what happened in those ones?" I couldn't think clearly.

"A prince climbs up Rapunzel's hair to get her out of the tower. Belle falls in love with a beast, and he turns back into a prince because she loves him," said Romy.

I couldn't see how these could apply to me. Wouldn't I need to have a beast and a prince and a tower to make those things happen?

"But why are these things happening to me now?" I asked. "If you did the spell when I was a baby?"

"Did you have a birthday recently?"

"Yeah . . . I turned thirteen last month."

"There you go, then. These things often kick in when you hit a milestone year."

I thought about all the CONGRATULATIONS! YOU'RE OFFICIALLY A TEENAGER birthday cards I'd gotten last month. None of them said WARNING! ANY SPELLS THAT WERE CAST ON YOU AS A BABY WILL ACTIVATE NOW.

"Make it stop," I said firmly to Madame Fredepia, who was puffing away on her cigarette. I pushed myself out of the sofa crevice and said it again, this time with a desperate whine in my voice. "You have to make it stop."

"I can't," she said, snuffing out her cigarette in a ruby-colored glass ashtray. "Even if I wanted to. The one who casts a spell cannot break it."

"But *you* did this!" I said. "You did all this to me."

"What about another spell?" asked Romy, grabbing my arm excitedly. She leaned so far forward off the sofa, she almost fell off it. "Could you do another one . . . like something more powerful than a counterspell?"

Something *more powerful* than a counterspell? What was she thinking? As if I didn't have enough going on. She wanted to layer another spell on top of the one I already had?

"No, no, too risky," said Madame Fredepia, shaking her head. "You can get unintended consequences when you multi-spell. The last person I did that to spoke with a squeak for a year. He sounded like a dog's chew toy."

"What about a prince, then?" asked Romy. "In fairy tales, princes are always breaking spells. You know, when they kiss the princess?" Romy squinted her eyes, and I could tell she was planning something. I wouldn't have put it past her to be plotting out a trek across Europe to find a prince for me.

"They do," said Madame Fredepia. "And that's exactly why that won't work for her. She's under a counterspell. Contrary forces are working on her. A prince can't rescue her. That's the whole point."

The words hit me like a blow. It wasn't as if I'd ever expected someone to save me, or that I even needed rescuing! But now being told that I could not be rescued, I felt suddenly terrified and helpless.

"You have to do something!" I wailed at Madame Fredepia. Why wasn't she trying to help me? She didn't seem like a mean woman. She sounded like she'd actually thought she'd been helping me and Mom when she cast her spells. But couldn't she now see that the counterspell was going to ruin my life? "You have to help me!"

"No," she said, speaking firmly and looking me level in the eyes. "You have to help yourself."

Chapter 9

ROMY'S HOUSE WAS THREE MILES ON THE other side of town, and she had another hour of cello practice on top of her homework to do, but she still walked me home. Best friends don't let you walk home alone when you've just realized that you're cursed and going to be sleepless for the rest of your life.

As we walked, pushing our bikes between us—we were both too distracted to cycle and talk at the same time—all the questions that I should have asked Madame Fredepia occurred to me. Which of the fairy tales would affect me? Would it include stories like "Hansel and Gretel" and

"Jack and the Beanstalk," even though I didn't think they had any princesses?

"What if she's wrong about everything?" asked Romy, stopping my train of thought, which was a good thing because that train was pulling into some strange stations. (Would the opposite of "Little Red Riding Hood" mean that I would try to eat my grandmother?) "She wasn't big on the details. Maybe the spell's just going to wear off."

"But what if it doesn't?" I moaned.

"Maybe it won't be that bad," said Romy. "You can become a shoe tycoon. Cia's Shoe Palace. You'll make a fortune."

"If I'm not getting kissed by frogs, or stuck under a pea and a pile of mattresses."

Sometimes Romy's relentless optimism was annoying. She always wanted to put a positive spin on things. Like if a teacher announced a pop quiz, Romy would say, *Guess we don't have to worry about this happening again tomorrow!* like that made everything okay. It's nice to have a best friend who believes the glass is always half full, but sometimes the glass really is half empty and you're so mad, you just want to smash it on the ground.

This was one of those times. I felt entitled to a full meltdown, and I was going to have it.

"That woman should be arrested," I began. "She should be in jail. I was just a baby! I don't want to worry that every time I open my locker, I'm going to get hit in the face by a shoe. And I want to be able to sleep like a normal person." I swiveled my bike around so that I was facing Romy. "And I don't understand how this all works . . . like, what about 'Rumpelstiltskin'? What's the opposite of that? And 'Jack and the Beanstalk'?"

I could hear my voice getting louder and shriller as I got more anxious. I needed to calm down, but I couldn't stop the panicky feeling that was racing through me.

"I hate frogs, Romy," I squeaked. "I don't want to have anything to do with frogs. Or anything slimy. And how long is this thing going to last? Till I get to high school? Or college? What if it never stops? What if this stuff just keeps happening to me forever?"

Romy walked toward me and gave me a hug, which was nice, but also a bit alarming—Romy is not a hugger.

"At least you don't have to worry about Indian fairy tales," said Romy softly. "Some of the princesses in those stories are really weird . . . like Kinnari. She has the head and body of a woman and the wings and feet of a swan. And then there's Yaksha, who eats lost travelers and—"

"This is not helping!" I said. Maybe I *did* have to worry about Indian fairy tales and being turned into a half swan, half girl. Madame Fredepia had said, *There are a lot of princesses.* How did I know which ones' stories were going to affect me?

"Well, I might have gotten it wrong," mused Romy. "It might have been the body of a swan . . . but I can ask my grandma. . . ."

"ROMY!"

"Sorry, Cia. But everything's going to be okay. Don't worry."

But I did worry. All the way home.

As soon as I got into my house, I ran to the mirror that hung on the wall beside our front door. Madame Fredepia's question about my hair kept looping around in my head on repeat. I really liked my hair. I got a lot of compliments about it. I stared at my reflection in the mirror, but my hair looked the way it always had. It was brown and curly and bouncy, and it skimmed my shoulders. Was it going to change color? Or go from curly to straight? Or would the strands turn into something else, giving me a Medusa-like head of wriggly snakes? At least from the front it still looked normal. I angled my head, but I couldn't get a look at the back of it.

"Riley!" I yelled. "C'mere."

Riley padded toward me. He was in his blue pajamas and looked like a mini lab technician. He was dressed for the job.

"Will you look at the back of my head?"

"Do you have nits?" he asked, his eyes widening with either excitement or disgust. There had been a lice out-break in his grade a few months ago.

"No, I don't," I said. "Will you just look at the back of my head?"

Riley stood on a chair and rolled up his sleeves. I bent my head toward him.

I felt his fingers on my head.

"What do you call a nit on a bald head?" he asked, laughing before he'd even given me the punch line. "Home-less!" Riley needed to work on his joke delivery. He never paused between the question and the answer. It all just came out together in one enthusiastic rush of words. He hit me with another one. "What do lice like to do all day? Knitting!"

"Riley." I wasn't in the mood for jokes. This was serious. "Do you see anything weird going on there? Anything unusual?"

"No," he said, running his hands through it. "You've got loads of hair. It's nice and soft. Like a sheep. Or a llama. Or a really soft dog. Or a soft cat. Or a monkey. Like a soft monkey butt."

"You're saying I have hair like a soft monkey butt," I said, laughing despite everything.

He jumped off the chair and slammed into my back, wrapping his arms around my neck and his legs around my waist.

"Piggyback!" he shouted.

I carried him to the kitchen. Dad was sitting at the counter eating a bowl of ice cream. Riley sidled up beside him. I grabbed a slice of leftover pizza.

"Hey, did you hear anything from Mom?" I asked. "I texted her earlier, but I couldn't get through."

"Sorry, love, nothing yet," said Dad, putting a scoop of rocky road into a bowl for Riley.

"When will she get back to the hostel?" I asked. Dad had said before that there was phone reception there.

"About seven p.m. in Tikopia, but it'll be the middle of the night here. You could try the hostel first thing in the morning. . . ."

I'll call her in the middle of the night, I thought, biting into my pizza. There were some advantages to not needing to sleep. And one of them was that it didn't matter what time zone the person you wanted to talk to was in.

In the meantime, I was going to check out the books on Mom's nightstand. Romy's comment about the princess in the Indian fairy tale who had swan wings and feet had freaked me out. Madame Fredepia had said that *whatever happened to the girls in fairy tales, the opposite, the contrary, will happen to you*. But which girls and which fairy tales was she talking about? Were Cinderella and Sleeping Beauty just the beginning of my nightmare? It was Mom's complaints about damsels in distress that had inspired Madame Fredepia to cast her spell, so if I could figure out which fairy-tale princesses Mom hated most, then maybe I'd know which ones I had to worry about.

"You all right, Cia?" asked Dad, looking up from his ice cream. "You look a bit . . ."

"Mad," noted Riley, sneaking a spoonful of ice cream from Dad's bowl.

"Well, just upset," corrected Dad. "Are you all right?"

"Yeah." I sighed. "Dad . . . that baby sleep-whisperer that Mom took me to . . ."

"You're not worried about that, are you?" asked Dad gently. "That was nearly thirteen years ago."

"No, it's just . . . why did Mom do it? Other moms, they'd take their babies to the doctor or they'd read a book about getting their baby to sleep. They wouldn't go to a . . ." I thought about how Madame Fredepia had changed her clothes and nail color in less than a minute, how she had ignited her cigarette with her fingers and told me she had made a "nice little spell" to get babies to sleep. "A witch."

"A witch!" laughed Dad. "Ah, Cia, don't be silly! Your mom didn't take you to a witch! Ah, no, she just needed a bit of help." His voice softened. "She was worried, Cia. She didn't know what she was doing. And she didn't have any sisters, no brothers who had gone through it already. She didn't have any family at all. No parents to give her advice."

I nodded. Mom was an only child whose parents had died before she and Dad met. I'd never thought about it, but of course that would have made being a new mom really hard. Though I still didn't think it made it okay for Mom to take parenting advice from a woman who spiked babies' bottles with aniseed and powdered newt's tail.

"And even if it was a witch, I'm sure it did you no harm at all!" joked Dad.

I started choking on my pizza. Dad whacked me on the back and gave me a glass of water.

Once Dad and Riley had fallen asleep, I went to the kitchen and made a cup of hot chocolate. I poured in the melatonin that Dad had gotten for me, and while it didn't make me sleepy, it gave the hot chocolate a nice, tart taste. I went back upstairs and, hot chocolate in hand, tiptoed into my parents' room. My dad was snoring loudly, sprawled across the bed like a shipwreck survivor washed up on the beach. I sat down on the edge of the bed, put my mug on Mom's bedside table, and looked at the books she had stacked there. There were about ten books—each one at least three hundred pages thick—about Chinese, Russian, Ghanaian,

Scandinavian, and Iroquois tales. I grabbed one called *The Folklore of Fairy Tales* for no reason other than that it had a nice cover. Most of the other books had at least one gruesome image—a crone with a single tooth, a giant with its massive hand around some poor guy's neck, a ferocious wolf with blood dripping from its mouth—on theirs. I started with a West African fairy tale about a girl named Chinye who sounded a bit like Cinderella—she had a nasty stepmother and stepsisters, but there was no prince. And Chinye didn't just outwit her mean relatives—she saved her village. I decided I didn't have to worry about her story and flipped through the rest of the pages. Mom wouldn't have been worried about the influence of this I-can-do-it-myself African princess, but should I worry about Yeh-Shen in China and Vasilisa in Russia and Niamh in Ireland and any of the other hundreds of fairy-tale princesses mentioned in these pages? It would take me hundreds of hours to read all the stories. I felt completely overwhelmed, like I was about to take a test that I hadn't studied for, and the effects of failing would be terrible.

Why hadn't I just asked Madame Fredepia what princesses Mom had been talking about?

My phone alarm beeped. I pulled my phone out of my robe pocket, worried that the noise would wake Dad, and turned it off. It was four a.m. A feeling of relief flooded me. I was going to talk to Mom.

Chapter 10

"TIKOPIA HOSTEL, GOOD EVENING," SAID A WOMAN with a strong accent. In the background there were noises, like pots and pans banging and a man shouting. Someone was burning the dinner.

"I'd like to speak to Professor Anderson, please. She's a guest there." I'd gone back downstairs and was standing in front of the mirror in the hallway. I angled my head, trying to get a better view of my hair. It seemed like it was okay, but I couldn't see the back.

"Just a moment, please," said the receptionist.

I thought about what I'd say when Mom got on the

phone. *Remember Madame Fredepia, whom you took me to when I was a baby? Well, she put a counterspell on me because of all that stuff you said about princesses, and now really weird things are happening to me, and I need to know which princesses you were complaining about, and . . .*

I heard the phone picking up.

"MOM!"

"I'm so sorry," said the same lady. "Professor Anderson has already left for the mainland."

My heart dropped. *And I'm scared.* That was the other thing I wanted to say to Mom. *I'm scared.*

After thanking the woman and hanging up, I walked into the kitchen and sat on a stool, trembling with anger and frustration and fear. Mom was the one who had gotten me into this mess, and I couldn't even talk to her to find out exactly how big of a mess I was in. What else could go wrong before I had a chance to talk to her?

I saw Riley's "best sister" picture on the counter. Looking at the goofy smile he'd drawn on my face and the oversized medal on my chest made me feel a tiny bit better. I thought about putting it in my room, but I'd probably see it more if it was in the kitchen. I took off the inspirational magnets Mom had put on the fridge door to make room for the picture, wondering, as I removed one that said YOU MUST EXPECT EXTRAORDINARY THINGS OF YOURSELF BEFORE YOU CAN DO THEM!, if she'd be thrilled that I had broken the world record for not sleeping and was walking around with a spell cast on me. Would she think that made me extraordinary? I definitely didn't. Not needing to sleep put me in the category of super-weird record holders like the poor man in Iowa who'd had hiccups for sixty-eight years. (I'd read about him in Riley's *Big Book of Outrageous Facts*.) And having a spell cast on you didn't mean you were extraordinary. It just meant you were really unlucky. I taped Riley's picture to the fridge door and stood back to admire it. It looked way better than those magnets.

For a moment, I thought about going back upstairs and continuing with *The Folklore of Fairy Tales*, but unless Mom had circled some of the fairy tales and written *Ugh!* I wouldn't be able to find what I was looking for. Then something occurred to me.

The box I'd opened in the attic earlier. It had Mom's research in it. I'd been born when she was in graduate school, so whatever she was researching about fairy tales then would have been on her mind when she visited Madame Fredepia. I felt a burst of excitement. It wasn't likely I'd find a top-ten list of Mom's most hated fairy-tale princesses, but checking out the contents of the box still seemed better than trawling through the mini library beside her bed.

In the attic, I found the box and pulled out a paper Mom had written called "Fairy-Tale Princesses and the Pointless Quest for the Happily Ever After." I skimmed through the pages, surprised that I agreed with everything that Mom had written. Why *hadn't* Cinderella kicked out her stepmother and stepsisters instead of cleaning up after them? Why did Snow White set herself up as a housekeeper for a pack of lazy dwarfs when she should have been figuring out how to get back at the Evil Queen? Mom's criticism went on and on—she was furious that Rapunzel spent all her time cleaning, and Belle reading, when they should have been working out how to escape their jailers. And then there was the Little Mermaid who gave up her voice and tail to get a pair of defective legs just so she could hang out with a cute guy. Mom was mad at her too.

I spread out the pages of Mom's work on the floor of the attic and let her words sink in, feeling sure that the fates of the princesses she had written about in this article were what Mom had wanted to protect me from when she met with Madame Fredepia almost thirteen years ago. The princesses were so helpless. If the counterspell meant that I would experience the opposite of what these fairy-tale princesses experienced, well, that would be a good thing, wouldn't it? I'd been feeling nothing but dread since I'd left Madame Fredepia's, but suddenly I felt hopeful. If the princesses were helpless and pathetic, then I'd be strong and—what was the opposite of pathetic? Excellent? That would be okay. I could handle that. Couldn't I?

About three hours later, after a breakfast of poached eggs and waffles, I cut through the high school parking lot on my way to school. I was looking forward to telling Romy that I had a short list of fairy-tale princesses to focus on and that she didn't need to get the details on any half-bird/half-human princesses from her grandma. Two girls in the parking lot caught my eye. They would have caught anyone's eye. They looked like they were on their way to a party on a fancy boat, not a day of classes. Even from far away I could spot their lash extensions, and they were wearing lipstick and layers of necklaces draped over their jackets. The pink Range Rover they were leaning against had a personalized license plate that said TRU LUV.

"Hey, you!" shouted one of the girls, smiling and flashing a mouth full of big white teeth at me.

"Hi," I said tentatively, slowing down my bike as I approached them. I looked from one girl to the other.

"I'm Hildee," said the first girl. Her eyelashes glistened when she blinked, and I realized they had tiny sparkly diamonds on the tips. "This is Wilhemina."

"We just want to say thank you," said Wilhemina. She covered her mouth and giggled. "You've really made her mad. She's had it too good for too long."

"Yeah," said Hildee, nodding her head so enthusiastically that her big hoop earrings banged against her chin. "It's not like she's even that pretty."

I didn't know who or what they were talking about, or who they seemed to think I was. "Um, I think you've mistaken me for someone else. I've gotta get to class," I said, putting my foot on the bike pedal.

The excited, almost starstruck way they were look-ing at me was kind of freaky. I wondered if they were on drugs.

"Bye," I said.

One of them shouted, "Have an awesome day. You've earned it!" as I biked away.

When I walked into school and turned down the hall-way to get to my locker, Romy came running toward me. Seeing the look on her face, I stopped, causing a brief pileup in the hallway.

"Did you hear about John Lee?" she asked, breathing heavily, as students grumbled and skirted around us. I offered her my water bottle, and she took a gulp.

I hadn't heard anything, but I braced myself for the breaking news that he had a girlfriend, feeling surprised that even with everything that was going on—like being the victim of a possibly unbreakable spell—I was still upset by the possibility that John Lee might like someone who wasn't me.

"He got some awful skin rash yesterday. Mia said she saw him at Yo-Yo Swirl last night and that he looked like a plague victim or something. She said his head was all swelled up and his eyes were bugging out."

"Poor guy," I said, feeling bad for John—but just a teeny bit relieved too. "Was it an allergic reaction?"

"They don't know why it happened, but he's in the hospital." She grimaced. "He's been there all night. Did your dad tell you about the email Mrs. Everley sent all the parents this morning? My mom just texted me about it."

I shook my head. My dad hadn't said anything about a message from the school, but he was usually a few days behind on emails.

"So, Mrs. Everley emailed the parents asking them to let the school know if any of us have signs of a rash or swelling," continued Romy, wrinkling her nose. "They're worried that there's something in the environment that might have caused John to just blow up like that." She blew air into her cheeks to show me, I guessed, what poor John must have looked like.

"That's terrible," I said as we approached our lockers. John was so sick that he was in the hospital, and they didn't even know what was wrong with him. That would be so scary.

"Yeah," said Romy, stopping in front of my locker. "Want me to open yours?" She placed the palm of her hand on it.

"Thanks, but I got it," I said, but I did feel nervous. I'd been wondering about what might hit me today. A hairbrush tsunami?

Romy stepped aside as I entered the lock combination and opened my locker a tiny bit. I peered inside. There was nothing on the floor of it other than my basketball shoes.

"It's okay," I said, reaching in to get my books for class.

"Aww," said Romy, looking into my locker. "I'm kind of disappointed. Still no size sixes?"

Rolling my eyes, I grabbed my books and headed to class.

During math, I sat down next to Raul Sheldon, who had a reputation for always knowing what was going on. If Raul had been around in colonial times, he would have beaten Paul Revere with the news that the British were coming by a couple of days. I'm not sure how he does it, if he just eavesdrops on conversations or reads his parents' emails or hacks into the school's computer system. Whatever it is, I'm pretty sure Raul's going to end up working for the CIA.

"Hey, Cia," he said. "So, this stuff about John . . ."

But then Mr. Martinez came into the class, banging the door behind him (he likes to make a dramatic entrance), and Raul stopped talking, meaning I never got to hear what he was going to say about John. My brain immediately went into overdrive, and I wondered if I should send him a get-well card or get his number from Raul and text him a GIF. Something funny, but one that also showed my sensitive side. . . . It would give us something to talk about when he got out of the hospital.

I tried to tune in to what Mr. Martinez was saying, but I kept thinking about what I could send John that wasn't too weird or cheesy. Plus, Mr. Martinez had the most boring, monotone voice. It was hard to listen to him when he spoke like he was trying to expend the least amount of energy possible. Back when I used to sleep, my eyes would get heavy during his class, and once or twice I had dozed off at my desk.

I leaned back in my chair and put my hands behind my

head. When I readjusted and moved my hands back to my desk, I saw that both of them were covered with my hair.

It was falling out.

The strands fell from my fingers onto the desk as I held back a scream. I glanced at Raul. His shoulders were sagging, and he was looking with half-open eyes at Mr. Martinez. He hadn't seen anything. I pushed the clumps of hair underneath my math book and tried to steady my breathing.

Was this what Madame Fredepia had been talking about? Did she know my hair was going to fall out? I felt a flash of fury. Why hadn't she warned me? This was the worst possible place for this to happen. Going bald in the middle of a math class! I put my head in my hands, and, very carefully, I rubbed my temples and the top of my head. Nothing fell out. But I couldn't just sit there and hope that I'd make it to the bell without shedding all over the desk. I raised my hand.

"Mr. Martinez," I said. "I really need to go the restroom."

I didn't wait for him to reply, just made for the door, walking sideways so that my classmates wouldn't see the back of my head. I didn't know how bad—how *bald*—things were back there. As soon as I got out of the room, I ran to the restroom across the hall and went to a sink. I shook my head over it, running my hands back and forth through my hair. When I looked down, the sink was full. There was enough of my hair in it to make Mr. Martinez a decent toupee. Maybe two toupees.

I let out a little whimper, feeling panic rising up inside me. Looking at myself in the mirror, my hair seemed okay from the front. I swiveled around, straining to peek over my shoulder, and saw a white tract of scalp on the back of my head.

I had a bald patch the size of an iPhone.

I scooped up the hair from the sink, threw it in a trash can, and stuffed some paper towels on top. I just knew that if Mia Johnson—who often used this restroom for her makeup tutorials—spotted the masses of curly brown hair in the trash, she'd be determined to find out who had put it there. She'd start questioning and scrutinizing every girl in our grade with curly brown hair (and there weren't that many of us), so in no time at all she'd figure out that it was me who was going bald. Then it would be all over the school, and students would talk in whispers around me and look at me with awful, pitying stares because they'd think I was sick. And the school counselor would stop me in the hallway to ask if I was okay and let me know her door was open all the time. It would be a nightmare. I shoved another fistful of paper towels into the trash can.

Then I ran into the last stall and locked the door. Pulling out my phone from my back pocket, I texted Romy. My hands were shaking.

Come to the girls' restroom. NOW. Beside Mr. Martinez's room.

As I sat and waited for Romy, I got more and more freaked out about the possibility that I'd have to go through middle school bald.

I didn't want to be bald. I needed my hair! I wasn't cool enough to pull off a shaved-head look. I pictured myself in a flouncy prom dress, with a bald head. How would I accessorize that? As the seconds passed, I got angrier and angrier with Madame Fredepia. She *knew* this was going to happen. Why hadn't she warned me?

"Cia!" shouted Romy, banging on the stall door. "What is going on?" She sounded breathless. She must have run all the way.

"I'm going bald," I said, opening the door.

"What?" said Romy, her face creasing with confusion.

I turned around.

Romy gasped. "What happened?"

"Madame Fredepia," I said, spitting out the syllables with disgust.

I turned back around so I was facing Romy.

"Remember she asked about my hair? Well," I shouted, pointing at my head, "this is what she meant. I'm losing my hair!"

"Look," said Romy, in a tone that I thought was far too calm given the dire situation. "We don't know if she actually did this to you. She just asked you how your hair was."

"*Rapunzel*," I whispered. "I figured it out last night. . . . The princesses I have to worry about . . . It's not just Cinderella and Sleeping Beauty. . . . It's Belle and the Little Mermaid and Snow White and *Rapunzel*."

I saw realization dawning on Romy's face. "Rapunzel's hair won't stop growing."

"And now I'm *bald*," I whimpered.

Romy put her hands on my shoulders and turned me around. "You are not bald."

"But I'm going to be," I moaned.

"You're not bald," repeated Romy firmly. "It's just a bald patch. We can cover it up. You've still got loads of hair . . . and even if you do lose your hair, you can just wear a wig."

I felt Romy pulling my hair back.

"It's a 'backover,'" she said, showing me a photo she had just taken of the back of my head.

It looked okay. She had bunched my hair together over the bald patch and tied it with my pink scrunchie into a messy bun. I couldn't see any scalp.

"Thank you," I said, reaching back and gingerly touching the bun. "This might work."

"Just don't mess with it too much," cautioned Romy. "Or, you know, run or jump around. If it falls out . . ."

Everyone will know I'm going bald.

I nodded. I'd have to fake a stomachache to get out of PE.

The rest of the morning was awful. I was so worried that the bun would fall apart that I was afraid to move my head, and I ended up walking and sitting in such a strained, stilted way that everyone kept asking me if I was okay.

Then during study hall, as I was eating a bag of chips

and sitting under the huge maple tree, a squirrel *pounced* on me.

Those things looked cute from a distance, but when you had one on your shoulder? It was a different story. There was nothing adorable about beady eyes and sharp teeth inches away from your face. I froze, terrified that it was going to go for my hair, but it reached down, grabbed my snack, and scampered back up the tree, making chirruping noises that sounded to me like *I've got your chips, I've got your chips.*

By the time I got to the cafeteria for lunch, I was annoyed and jittery and ready to go home. Maybe it was just me, but I felt like there was a tense atmosphere hanging over the lunch tables. Little clusters of teachers huddled together, talking in hushed tones, and Mrs. Everley, the school principal—whom I never saw in the cafeteria—was striding purposefully around the room barking orders at Mr. Solomon, the school janitor, who was gripping a clipboard and looking terrified.

I got a chocolate milk and a sandwich from the lunch line and sat down at an empty table, scanning the crowd for Romy.

Before I could find her, Roger Wu came lumbering toward me with his head thrown back and his arms outstretched, like he was doing a Frankenstein impersonation. What was wrong with him? I looked down and took a bite of my sandwich, hoping he'd sit somewhere else.

"Cia, help me!" he yelled. "It's too dark! I can't see anything!" His arms flailed around my head. "Shine bright and lead me out of the dark."

He was quoting that ridiculous note that Mom had left in my backpack. Some kids at the next table—a group of eighth graders—started laughing.

He stalked off, yelling over his shoulder, "Cia, you are strong and powerful!"

Romy sat down beside me.

"Roger Wu is such a jerk," I said through gritted teeth.

"Don't worry about him," said Romy dismissively. "You've got bigger things to think about."

"Like going bald?" I sighed, wondering if I should have thrown my milk in Roger's face. I would've been sent to the principal's office, but it might have been worth it. He'd be a complete nightmare if I did end up with no hair.

I could just imagine him yelling, *Cia, you are strong and powerful and bald!*

"No," said Romy, pausing and dropping her voice. "Cia, something's happened." She sounded so serious that I immediately stopped thinking about Roger Wu dripping wet with chocolate milk and held my breath.

"What?"

"It's John," she said. "An infectious disease specialist from the CDC has arrived to examine him. Raul just told me about it."

"The CDC?" I gulped. The Center for Disease Control, the big government agency that gave out vaccines and stuff, was checking out John? This was not good. "Someone from the government has come to look at John?"

"Yeah," confirmed Romy. "And there's talk about closing the school if the CDC doctor thinks John might be contagious."

I glanced over at a nearby table of teachers. Was that why they looked so stressed? Were they worried that the school was contaminated with something awful?

"Raul says . . ." Romy paused and swallowed. "Raul

says that John's 'got tufts of hair growing on his face now,' along with the swelling . . . says he's starting to look 'like a bit of a beast.'"

"A . . . what?"

"A bit of a beast," repeated Romy. She stared at me for a long moment and then looked at the table.

John Lee—the only boy whom I'd ever had a crush on—was, if reports were to be believed, becoming a beast.

"Oh no," I said. I felt like I was going to be sick. I pushed away my grilled cheese. "What have I done?"

"We don't know if this has anything to do with you," said Romy, but I could tell by the intense expression on her face that she didn't believe that. The same thought that just struck me was occurring to her, too. This had everything to do with me and the counterspell.

"I've turned John Lee into a beast," I said.

I looked around the cafeteria at all the other students, just being students. Eating their lunches, laughing, talking, messing around. One boy was not here because of me. One boy was in the hospital because of me. A sense of shame flooded me. It was one thing for me to lose my hair and not need to sleep and handle massive amounts of shoes popping up in inconvenient places, but this was different. This was another person.

Sure, I wasn't responsible for the spell that had started it all, but I was responsible for John being stuck in the hospital, being analyzed by government agents, and sprouting hair in all the wrong places. My crush had made that happen.

"In 'Beauty and the Beast,' Belle loves the beast, and her love turns him back into a man," I said to Romy, hoping that if I said what was in my head, it wouldn't seem as bad. "And I . . ."

No, it was as bad. It was terrible.

"And you . . . ," continued Romy delicately.

"And I . . ." I gulped. "I like John Lee."

I let that hang there for a moment.

"And the opposite, the counter, of the 'Beauty and the Beast' story is that my liking him is turning him into a—"

I couldn't say it.

"A beast," said Romy grimly.

"Oh no," I said, groaning so loudly that Delaney Allen, a seventh grader who was sitting at the next table, looked over at us, eyed the grilled cheese in front of me, and then looked suspiciously at the one on her plate.

"I think this might actually be good," whispered Romy, leaning closer to me.

"Good?" I gasped in disbelief. Did Romy not remember what the beast in "Beauty and the Beast" looked like? He was huge. He was hairy. Sported big fangs and scary claws. He was called a beast for a reason.

I stared at Romy. Her eyes were squinting with the effort of thinking. I could almost see her mind working, looking for a positive angle to spin.

"I've got it," she gasped in the manner of a scientist making a groundbreaking discovery. "I know what you need to do."

"What?"

"I know how you can break the spell," said Romy excitedly. "John turning into a beast . . ." She grinned. "It's the best thing that could have happened!

"Well, not to him, obviously," she continued, taking in my horrified expression. "But it is for you. . . . Cia, now you have a way to break the spell. You can break the counterspell!"

Out of the corner of my eye, I saw Delaney Allen

looking at us with her mouth hanging open. "Just rehearsing for the play!" I shouted at her, hoping that she had never examined the plot of *Romeo and Juliet* in any great detail.

"Romy, keep your voice down," I hissed, scanning the cafeteria to make sure no one else was looking at us.

"Sorry," whispered Romy. "It's just, I'm excited. It's so obvious, Cia. John just needs to kiss you, and that'll break the spell."

"What?" Me? Kiss John Lee? Sure, I'd spent months daydreaming about talking to him, imagining that we'd have such an amazing conversation that he'd ask me to go to Yo-Yo Swirl after school and everyone would turn around and stare at us when we walked in together. . . . But kissing him? I hadn't even let myself think about that. I could feel the heat of a blush starting to bloom on my face.

"You have to do it, Cia," said Romy urgently. "Think about it. . . . In 'Beauty and the Beast,' Belle saved the beast when she kissed him, and you'll save John when . . ." She paused. "When *he* kisses you."

"Hang on," I said, pushing away an image that had popped into my head of me with my eyes closed, face upturned, waiting for John's kiss. "But remember how Madame Fredepia specifically said a prince can't rescue me?"

"Yep," said Romy decisively. "A prince can't rescue you. But John's not a prince, and he's not going to rescue *you*; you're going to rescue *him*. You'll be turning him back to normal. That's what makes this so perfect."

I sighed. What was happening to John was my fault, and I had to do something to help him. If there was a chance that this kissing thing would break the spell, then I had to try it. But I hated the idea of waltzing into John's hospital room and—what?—demanding that he kiss me? What if he didn't want to kiss me? Maybe if I explained to him that he was turning into a beast because of a spell and that this was the only way to break it, he'd want to kiss me then, wouldn't he? Unless he didn't believe in magic or he thought I was completely repulsive. I lifted my hand up to check on my hair.

"How's my bun?" I asked Romy.

"Good." She nodded. "Now, how are we going to get to the hospital?"

"What about Noah?" I suggested. "He still owes us for helping with his project." Noah was Romy's older brother and the nicest guy. He was in film school, and a few weeks ago we'd helped him out with a class assignment by dressing up as bandits and throwing bananas at each other. It had been fun for a while, but not after Noah had made us do it about a million times so he could get the perfect shot for the silent comedy he was making. He definitely owed me and Romy.

"Yeah," said Romy. "I'll ask him now." She pulled out her phone. "I'll see if he'll take us after school."

My palms were sweating already. Just thinking about walking into the hospital was freaking me out. At least I had picked a cute outfit today. A denim mini and a lavender sweatshirt.

Romy's phone beeped. "Noah can take us. He'll meet us outside school."

"Okay," I said, a nervous feeling growing in my stomach. I was really going to do this. I'd never said more than two words to John Lee, and in a few hours, I was going to march into his hospital room and tell him he needed to kiss me.

"This is going to be great," said Romy, smiling at me as she packed up her lunch box. "You're going to break that spell, Cia."

Or, I thought, die of embarrassment trying.

Chapter 11

THE TWO CLASSES AFTER LUNCH PASSED IN A blur. I kept thinking about how I'd approach the kissing thing with John, if I should just stride into the hospital room and, by way of greeting, lean over and kiss him on the cheek. But there was no guarantee that he would reciprocate, and it was also totally cringey. I wondered about asking Mia Johnson for a quick makeover—a bit of lip gloss and mascara, nothing dramatic—because I thought that maybe I should try to look as nice as possible, but she'd want to know what had caused my sudden interest in makeup, and I'd seen enough Mia Johnson

makeovers to know that she always interrogated the girl being transformed about which boys she liked. No, I decided, I couldn't risk it. I'd start blushing, and everyone in the grade would know I had a crush on someone.

I checked my phone just before my last class and saw that Mom had called three times. I felt relieved that she had cell service again, annoyed that I had missed her, and confused about whether or not I should call her back. I wasn't nearly as angry with her as I'd been last night, and I'd already figured some things out for myself. I wondered if I should call her to run my spell-breaking plan by her—she was a fairy-tale expert, after all—but I couldn't tell my mom I was going to beg a boy to kiss me. She'd be totally horrified. I didn't want to have that conversation. I shoved my phone into my backpack and headed to class.

My last class of the day, science with Mrs. Taylor.

"Yo, Cia," said Gavin. He had a pair of lab goggles on his head, a pencil stuck behind each ear, and a bit of whatever he had had for lunch on his chin.

"You've got something . . ." I touched my chin.

"Right, thanks," he said, wiping his face with the back of his hand.

I pulled up a stool and sat beside him. I'd forgotten that we were dissecting earthworms today. There were five dried-up, long-dead specimens in a glass tube on the table in front of us. Every student in the class had been given a few to work with.

Later on, the school administration would point to the abundance of worms in the seventh grade science lab as an explanation for the bizarre, terrifying incident that led to Mrs. Taylor's early retirement, the destruction of almost all the lab equipment, and the attack on a middle school student. But that was later.

"Good afternoon," began Mrs. Taylor. "You're all going to do a worm dissection today. And before anyone asks—" She paused and looked pointedly at Rebecca Harrison, who had stopped the dissection of a chicken wing a few weeks ago to ask whether or not what we were doing was entirely ethical. (She had had a point.) "All these worms have had a lovely long life," continued Mrs. Taylor. "In the best of soil. And died of natural causes."

There were twitters of laughter from the class and a loud "yeah, right" from Rebecca Harrison. Mrs. Taylor ignored it and walked over to a window. She opened the top part.

"It's very hot in here," she muttered, returning to her desk. "Safety first," she said, this time looking pointedly at Gavin. "Put on the goggles, aprons, and plastic gloves before you start."

I suited up, adjusting the goggles to the widest fitting so I could maneuver the strap gently around my bun.

"Now, put a worm on the dissecting tray, dorsal side-up, and count the segments and find the setae," said Mrs. Taylor as she walked around the room.

Gavin held up the glass tube, and I lifted a worm out using the tweezers.

"What's the setae?" he asked me.

I was about to answer when a bird landed on my arm. A big, overweight pigeon. I screamed. Why was a bird sitting on me?

"What the . . . ," gasped Gavin, as another bird landed on top of me. It staked out a spot on my head.

I stood up and tried to shake the two birds off, but the more I moved, the more their claws pressed into me. I resisted the urge to scream again. Some instinct was telling me to be still, to stay as calm as possible. I looked frantically around the lab trying to figure out where the birds had come from.

"Mrs. Taylor!" shouted Gavin.

She turned around, the annoyed look on her face rapidly changing to shock when she saw what was happening at our workstation. She ran to the open window, arms up, ready to close it, but she didn't make it in time. Twenty more birds streamed through the window, pushing her back. She screamed and fell to the ground. Students jumped up from their stools yelling and ran for cover underneath their tables. Some of them threw petri dishes, dissection trays, and books at the birds. I saw Rebecca Harrison, concern for animal welfare forgotten, take down three pigeons with a well-aimed stool.

All the birds headed for my table. And within seconds they were all over me, five on each arm, one on each shoulder, and two—possibly three—on my head. There was a lot of movement up there—the pigeons' claws and beaks pulled at my hair—and I had to resist the urge to jump up and down to shake them off. I took tiny sips of air in case breathing too heavily irritated them. The ones that couldn't find a perch on top of me landed on my workbench, their twitchy heads moving from side to side, but they never took their small black eyes off me. They almost looked like they were trying to say something to me.

I thought about the fairy tales I had read. How did birds fit into those? Didn't birds mend Cinderella's old dress and help Snow White clean the dwarfs' filthy house? Or maybe that was just the Disney versions. These birds didn't look like those sweet delicate fluff balls. These birds were big, lumbering creatures, swooping through the air knocking down Bunsen burners. And they had mean, beady eyes. But it wasn't their eyes that terrified me; it was their beaks. There were at least twenty of them pointed in my direction. I felt like a character in an action movie with a bomb strapped to me. One false move and I'd be blown (or, in this case, pecked) to smithereens.

I felt something grab my leg. I swiveled my eyes toward the ground. It was Mrs. Taylor, sweaty, panting, and wild-eyed. "I'll get help," she gasped. Even though the birds didn't seem interested in anything or anyone other than me, Mrs. Taylor was staying low to the ground. She moved away on her elbows and knees as if she were crawling through a war zone.

As a pigeon on my shoulder got alarmingly close to

my earlobe, I remembered something from the stories I'd flipped through last night—there was a chance that these birds were here to help me, or to deliver an important, yet hard to understand, message. Then again, there was also a chance that they just wanted to poke my eyes out.

I decided to say something, channeling Cinderella and Snow White and what they would have done in this situation. I directed my question to the two birds on the countertop, trying to speak in a princess-like, sweet-as-apple-pie voice.

"May I help you?"

Either I asked the wrong question, or they found my princess impression offensive.

The birds attacked me. They went straight, as I had feared, for the eyes, their beaks bouncing off the safety goggles' glass visor.

I ran toward the door but tripped over Mrs. Taylor, who had almost made it out to the hallway. I went down, hard, and stayed on the ground, placing my hands over my head as birds dive-bombed me from above. The door out of the lab was just a few feet away. If I could make it through it and then out to the hallway, I could race to the home economics room and slam the door shut before they could follow me in. Crawling toward the door, I braced myself for a barrage of pecks but instead felt a stream of cold liquid on my head and heard a whooshing roar. I looked up and saw Gavin, fire extinguisher in hand, standing in the middle of a haze of white smoke. With the goggles, lab coat, and manic look in his eyes, he looked like a Ghostbuster.

"I'll cover you!" he shouted over the noise of cooing and flapping, students screaming, and the fire alarm that Mrs. Taylor must have pulled before collapsing on the floor beside me. "I'll get 'em out!" He yelled at Rebecca Harrison to open all the windows.

I scooted to the door, reached up to open it, and made it out into the hallway, slamming the door behind me.

Gavin managed to clear the room of pigeons before the fire trucks and ambulances arrived. Mrs. Taylor was taken away in one of them to be treated for shock.

I had scratches all over my hands, was soaking wet, and had—as far as everyone else could see—lost large amounts of hair during the bird attack. The birds actually hadn't done too much damage; they'd just ripped apart the messy bun, revealing the bald patch that I'd been trying to hide. Mrs. Everley, who was running down the hallway just as I emerged from the science lab, went pale when she saw me and insisted that I go to the nurse's office.

"School's under attack!" shouted Raul to no one in particular as he passed me on my way to the nurse's office. I weaved my way through throngs of excited students as almost equally excited teachers tried to corral them into a classroom. I kept my head down and a hand up to cover my bald patch.

Romy was at the nurse's office when I got there.

"Cia! I just saw Mrs. Everley. I heard what happened," she said, eyes wide. "Are you okay?"

"Yeah," I answered, pulling the goggles off my head. "It looks worse than it is."

Mrs. Gaskin put ointment and bandages on my hands while Romy looked in the lost-and-found bin for some clothes that would fit me.

"Sorry, this was the best I could do," she said, holding out a pair of jeans and a kid's-sized blue T-shirt that had somehow found its way into the lost-and-found bin at our middle school. It had DON'T CALL ME PRINCESS! emblazoned on the front of it.

"They're fine," I said.

I stepped into the alcove in the nurse's office and got changed, turning the shirt inside out so the letters wouldn't show. I threw my drenched miniskirt and lavender sweatshirt into a plastic bag. So much for my cute outfit.

When I came back out, Romy threw a New York Knicks baseball cap at me.

"Thanks," I said, putting it on my head.

We were leaving the nurse's office when Raul came running up to us.

"John update," he panted, doubling over to catch his breath.

I wondered if he'd been running around the school shouting out news alerts the whole time we'd been in the nurse's office.

"He's in quarantine," said Raul, straightening up. "Full lockdown quarantine."

"What does that mean?" I asked, my heart skipping a beat. I knew what quarantine meant. I just needed some time to process what Raul was telling us.

"No one can get in to see him," said Raul. "The CDC people are worried that whatever John's got is contagious and not treatable."

No visitors. This was terrible.

I had had enough. I just wanted everything to be over—the not sleeping, the footwear, the hair loss, and now the bird attack. Things were not just getting stranger; they were getting dangerous. John Lee's hairy, beastly situation had gotten so bad, a government agency had *quarantined* him. I had to do something.

I turned to Romy. One way or another, I was getting in to see John Lee and breaking the spell.

"Let's go."

Chapter 12

ROMY AND I WALKED OUTSIDE THE SCHOOL GATES just as her older brother, Noah, pulled up in his car.

"Hop in the back, guys." Noah leaned out the driver's window. "The front seat's full of my camera stuff."

I opened the car door, knowing that every eighth-grade girl in the area—plus whatever high schoolers might be around and even a few of the teachers, too—would have their eyes glued to Noah Agarwal. When he came to the school a couple of months ago to see Romy's cello recital, he almost caused a stampede.

Basically, Noah Agarwal is gorgeous. My mom, who

never comments on how anyone looks, always says *That young man is a movie star* whenever she sees Noah. But she says it while shaking her head, like having a perfect smile and a chiseled jaw and broad shoulders is some kind of curse.

Mia Johnson walked out of the school gates, stopped dead in her tracks when she caught sight of Noah, and immediately started applying lip gloss. I couldn't resist giving her a little wave as we drove by.

Noah, like everyone in Romy's family, is really kind, and smart. He might be the best-looking guy in the tri-state area, but to me he's just Romy's big brother whom I've known since I was eight.

"So, I'm taking you two to Mount Carmel?" said Noah, glancing over his shoulder. "Nice of you two to visit your classmate. . . ."

"Thanks, Noah," I said, wondering how much Romy had told him about John.

Mount Carmel, the hospital where John had been admitted, was almost ten miles away. Romy and I had a little over ten minutes to come up with a plan.

"You could pretend you have the same thing John has. . . ."

"What? That I'm getting bigger and hairier?" I asked. "That's not going to work." I pointed at my balding head that was still covered by the hat.

"Okay," said Romy, not missing a beat. "How about we pull a fire alarm to create a distraction and you run in and find the supply room—"

"What are you two talking about?" interrupted Noah, who turned around to give us a suspicious look as we waited at a red light.

"School project," Romy and I said at the same time.

"I don't know what you two are up to," said Noah, narrowing his eyes. "But just so you know, you can get a year in prison for pulling a fire alarm. So, you might want to leave that bit out."

Romy grunted, folded her arms, and scowled at Noah. But I thought he'd made a good point.

"Don't want to have to visit you in jail, sis," he said good-naturedly, turning back to look at the road. "You neither, Cia."

He pulled the car into the hospital parking lot and stopped in front of the main entrance.

"Just text me when you're ready to go," he said.

Romy and I thanked him before we got out of the car and walked toward the big double doors.

"Let's do this," said Romy determinedly.

"I'm going in alone," I said, realizing as soon as I heard myself speaking that I sounded ridiculously dramatic. "I just mean I don't want you getting into trouble." Romy snorted dismissively. "And I think," I continued, "for this to actually work . . . you know, to actually break the spell, that I have to do it on my own."

I'd been thinking more about the fairy tales on the drive over.

"So, if I'm sort of the 'prince'—you know, the one doing the rescuing—well, then I should be like one of those princes in the fairy tales. And they never have a best friend with them. Like the prince in 'Sleeping Beauty' and the one in 'Snow White'—they turn up on their own. . . ."

"Yeah," said Romy, looking thoughtful. "You're right. The prince in 'Rapunzel' climbs up the tower on his own. . . ."

"Doesn't have a best friend on the ground cheering him on . . . ," I added.

"I could just wait outside John's room while you run in and, you know, get the kiss."

"No," I said, becoming more certain that going in alone was the right thing to do. I didn't want Romy—even if she was my best friend—waiting on the other side of the door while I was trying to persuade John to kiss me.

"Okay," said Romy, looking resigned. "How are you going to get them to let you in, though?" She pointed at the reception area behind the double doors.

"I'll just try to sneak in, then," I said, ignoring Romy's look of disbelief. She knew I'd never tried to sneak in anywhere. Had never even tried to cut the lunch line. "I could pretend to be with another family . . . you know, like, just sort of walk in beside them . . ." I scanned the parking lot to see if there were any likely visitors heading into the hospital, ideally with a ton of kids. The receptionist wouldn't notice another one, right?

"Maybe you could use magic!" said Romy.

"What?" I gasped. "Romy, I don't have any magic."

"You might," she said. "You've been spelled, so that might make you, I don't know, a bit magicky. Just go in and stare at the receptionist and tell them that you have to see John Lee. Just sort of mesmerize them."

"You mean hypnotize them," I said.

"Yeah," she said, eyes lighting up. "That's it, hypnotize them—you don't even need to have magic to do that. Just focus and hypnotize them into letting you see John Lee."

Romy's can-do optimism had reached a new level of wishful thinking.

"Romy," I said, trying not to sound annoyed. It would be amazing if things really worked that way, if by just thinking something, by just wanting something enough, you could make it happen. Sometimes it seemed like that's what Romy believed, but I didn't. You couldn't turn yourself into a hypnotist just because you really wanted to be able to hypnotize someone. "I can't hypnotize anyone."

"But . . ."

"You know what," I said, turning away from her and walking toward the entrance. "I'm just going to do this." The double doors slid open as I approached. I couldn't look back at my best friend, or else I might not be able to go through with it.

"I'm here to see John Lee," I said to the man sitting behind the front desk. "He's a patient here."

"Let's see . . . John Lee," said the man, looking down at his computer. "He's not allowed any visitors."

"You *want* to let me see John Lee," I said in my most persuasive voice, hoping for the best. I felt like an idiot, and I could tell from the way the man was looking at me that he thought I was one too.

"All righty," he said. "But you can't see John Lee. Patient's in quarantine. Doesn't matter what I want." He looked back down at his computer.

Rejected.

There was a gift shop just beside the double doors, and I stepped inside it to give myself a moment. I needed some time to think before trying something else or giving up and heading back out to Romy. I wouldn't put it past her to tell me that I should try to levitate up to the hospital's second floor and get in through a window.

From the doorway of the gift shop, I could see the reception desk and the double doors behind it. I watched two women approach the desk and talk to the man behind it, and then the double doors swung in and they walked through to the main part of the hospital. Through the open doors, I could see into the hallway beyond and spotted the bank of elevators at the end.

The elevator in the middle was different from the others. Framed in wrought iron, it looked more like an ornate gateway to Narnia or something rather than an elevator.

It was an elevator, but it was something more, too.

I hung out in the gift shop for a bit longer, watching. Every time the double doors swung open, I had a few seconds to see the elevator. None of the visitors used it, instead choosing ones on either side of it.

Finally, I realized what I was looking at. It was a gateway to a castle. The iron trelliswork, the banner in the middle—it looked like something from a storybook.

If John was turning into a beast, wasn't it possible that the hospital where he had been "imprisoned," or just the room he was in, was turning into a castle? And if so, how did that change my chances of getting in to see him?

I thought about the "Beauty and the Beast" story. What did I know about the castle? It had been enchanted—that was for sure. Belle's father had thought it was empty and sheltered there during a storm, and the next morning he plucked a red rose from the garden to give to Belle, and that made the beast so angry that he tried to lock up the old man—or kill him, depending on which version of the story you read. But then the Beast agreed to let the man go if he'd send a daughter back in his place. So really, it was the taking of the rose that got the "Beauty and the Beast" story moving.

I had an idea. It was ridiculous, but it was better than nothing.

I looked around the gift shop, finding what I was looking for in a bucket beside the magazine rack. It wasn't exactly what I wanted, but it was close enough. I paid the cashier and ran back outside to where Romy was waiting.

"What's that for?" she asked.

"This," I said, holding up a single red carnation, "is how I'm going to get in."

Chapter 13

I EXPLAINED MY PLAN TO ROMY.

"I need you to distract the guy at the front desk, though," I said. "I think he'll stop me if I walk through the doors behind him."

"No problem," said Romy. With determined strides, she began heading toward the doors.

I followed her in. I owed her an extra-large yogurt at Yo-Yo Swirl.

Romy walked up to the receptionist desk, fell on top of it, and then slid on to the ground as if she had just fainted.

It was possibly more dramatic than necessary, but

it did the trick. The man jumped up and peered over his desk to look at Romy on the ground. I walked by as quickly as I could without breaking into a run, holding the carnation in front of me like I was a relay runner about to pass the baton. The doors swung open, and I didn't break stride until I reached the elevators. Stopping in front of the castle entrance elevator, I held up the flower.

The doors parted and I stepped inside. I resisted the urge to peek out before the doors closed, terrified that I'd see a security guard charging toward me. There was a single large button on a panel that lit up the number 8 as the doors slid together. With a creaking groan, the elevator began to move upward.

I exhaled with relief and looked around, wondering if there was anything else I should be noticing. Was there anything in the elevator that might help me get into John's room? I thought about the talking candlestick in the Disney movie. . . . What if there was one of those in here? He'd be really helpful.

I checked out all the corners. Nothing. I was the only one in the elevator.

The interior was beautiful, with hundreds of

miniature gilded mirrors lining the ceiling and fabric wallpaper embossed with tiny roses. I wondered, feeling a teeny bit excited for the first time since all this began, if I'd be stepping out into the grounds of a castle. Maybe the eighth floor of the hospital had been transformed into a courtly maze.

The elevator jerked to a halt, the doors opening swiftly, and I was pitched forward out onto a regular-looking hospital floor. There didn't seem to be any transformation going on up here. As I steadied my stumble and snapped out of daydreaming, I remembered that this was a restricted area. I wasn't supposed to be here. Was I breaking the law? Noah said Romy and I could go to prison for pulling a fire alarm—was this a bigger crime than that? My stomach twisted with fear, but I breathed through it. I just needed to work fast. Get in, get the kiss, and get out.

I saw a sign for a row of rooms. The number 806 was decorated with roses. After placing my carnation on the floor of the elevator just before it closed, I started walking toward room 806, sticking close to the wall and keeping my head down so that I wouldn't draw attention to myself. The hallway was empty except for a large man who I guessed to be John's dad standing outside room 806 talking on the phone. He was definitely big enough to be Mr. Lee. I remembered hearing that he had been a professional football player for a while. I stepped into an alcove just beside the room, waiting for him to leave—go to the restroom? get some fresh air?—so that I could get into the room.

"Looks like they're figuring this thing out," he said into the phone. "They've ruled out radiation poisoning. Doctor thinks it's being caused by a surge of testosterone. . . . That'd explain the hair and the growth spurt . . . so it's gotta mean there's something going on with the pituitary gland." He broke off. The person on the other end must have been talking. "Yeah, yeah," he continued. "Just need some more tests. Specialist said the hardest part is coming up with the right diagnosis. . . ."

John's dad checked his watch and said, "I'm going to grab a coffee." He put his phone in his back pocket and walked toward the elevators.

This was it. This was my chance. John Lee was on the other side of that door. My heart was hammering so hard, I felt like I might pass out. I balled my hands into fists and willed myself to calm down and breathe slowly. Wishing

I was still wearing the cute outfit I started the day with, I tucked my T-shirt into my jeans, then changed my mind and took it out. I removed the baseball cap and touched my hair. It was still a bit wet from the soaking Gavin had given me, and I figured it was probably better to keep the hat on anyway, just in case I started shedding again.

I was terrified. How was John going to react when I walked into the room? I reminded myself that he had walked across the cafeteria to give me my scrunchie, and that he had smiled at me in science. *He likes you, Cia*, I told myself, *or at least he doesn't* not *like you. Just do this.*

I knocked on the door. When there was no answer, I pushed it open slowly and stepped into the room.

John, or what used to be John, was sitting up in the bed. It looked like the transformation from seventh-grade boy to fairy-tale monster was about halfway done. Even though I had known a bit of what to expect, I couldn't help staring at the massive, hairy beast in front of me.

John was now as tall and wide as his father and filled every inch of the bed, meaning that he had grown about a foot both horizontally and vertically in just a day. He had a shaggy brown beard that covered the lower half of his face, and his hair was so long that it was impossible to tell where it ended and the beard began. How could his parents and the doctors not see it? Put a puffy white shirt and blue velvet jacket on him, and he could audition for the live-action movie role. He looked way worse than I'd imagined. I'd been expecting him to look weak and sick and hairy, and he did look hairy, but he didn't look ill. He looked strong and he looked scary, and somehow, that seemed worse than looking sick.

"Cia?" said John in his normal voice (had I been expecting a growl?), sounding surprised but not—I noticed, feeling a little thrill—annoyed or disappointed. He pushed himself up on the bed with his huge hairy forearms.

It was all John, John Lee. The boy who had crossed the cafeteria to bring my scrunchie was still there. My heart jumped when he said my name, and I felt a ridiculous sense of satisfaction that he had remembered it. (Why would he have forgotten it? He didn't have a concussion.)

"How did you get in? They said they weren't letting me have visitors."

"Well, they let me in," I said, as casually as I could, as

if I was so confident and amazing that security guards everywhere just waved me in. I tossed my head back, then immediately regretted it. Why was I tossing my head? My hair was covered up with a baseball cap! In the awkward pause that followed, I realized I was still standing next to the closed door, and I wondered if I should sit on the chair beside John's bed. I took a step closer, hoping he'd invite me to sit down.

He didn't.

I wished for the millionth time that I was still wearing my cute skirt and lavender sweater and not the terrible T-shirt and baggy jeans—that I was starting to suspect were meant for boys—and I wished that I could pull off the black baseball cap. I should have asked for that makeover from Mia. Now that I was here—badly dressed and completely terrified—the idea of just telling John the truth and asking him to kiss me seemed even more impossible.

"So, how are you feeling?" I stalled, feeling a surge of sympathy for him. He was barely fitting into the bed.

"I feel pretty good, actually. I've got, like, this super-strength now." John grabbed a thick paperback book off the table beside his bed. It looked like a three-hundred-pager.

He held it in both hands and then ripped it in two, right down the middle of the cover, like it was a single sheet of paper, before flinging both halves on the floor.

My shock must have shown on my face—why would he destroy a perfectly good book?!—because he looked right at me and sort of sneered.

"It's Dad's. He won't care. He's so freaked out about all this." He pointed at his face, but really, he could have pointed at any part of himself. *All* of him looked freaky. "I can do pretty much anything, and he won't get mad at me." He took the can of Coke that was on the table and drank out of it, then crushed the can and threw that on the floor beside the remains of the paperback. "I can just eat and drink and do whatever I want. And no school. So, yeah, I'm good."

Why was John acting this way? I'd never visited anyone in the hospital before—maybe people just got frustrated from having to stay in bed all the time and sometimes acted out.

John grabbed his phone.

"I heard about what happened in science class," he said, tapping on the screen. It looked tiny in his massive hands. He still had hands, not paws, though his finger-nails were alarmingly long and curved, and it looked like he was having trouble with the touch screen.

I relaxed. He was going to ask me if I was okay. Then he'd tell me that that must have been really scary, and maybe he'd even say—or at least *think*—that I was brave. This would be good. This would give us something to talk about. . . .

"My phone's been blowing up with texts." He looked down at his screen, and I thought I saw the stubby begin-nings of a pair of horns on the crown of his head. "Roger posted a video on Instagram."

"Roger Wu?" I asked, feeling my guard go up.

"Yeah," said John. "That dude's awesome."

Awesome? Roger Wu was a jerk. How could John think he was cool? I felt my heart drop to my stomach. Roger was . . . mean.

"So, is it just birds that don't like you, or all animals?" John said, laughing in a condescending way. "What about dogs? You ever get bitten by a dog?"

"No," I said, annoyed that my voice was shaking. Why was John acting this way? Was he laughing at me?

"Is there anything left up there?" He pointed at my head. "Or did the pigeons pull it all out?"

I felt myself blush and touched my baseball cap. Then I got upset that I cared about John's opinion of my hair.

"I don't think you've got what it takes to do the no-hair look," he said, pulling his eyes away from his phone and staring at me. "Only good-looking, confident girls can do that."

The words stung so much that I felt like I'd been slapped. John Lee had just told me that he didn't think I was cute.

No, it was worse than that. He didn't think I was confident, either. He thought I was ugly and timid. I felt a wave of humiliation wash over me. He didn't like me. He'd never liked me.

"You gotta see Roger's video," he said. "It's so funny. You're like a bird magnet or something. I think a couple pooped on you."

My heart started racing so fast, I could feel the blood pulsing behind my temples. Was John always this mean? Was he always this much of a jerk? Had the cute dimples and his great hair blinded me to what he was really like? Was he as cruel as Roger Wu? After John had dropped off my scrunchie, had he told Roger how I'd blushed and been totally weird when he approached my table? Had the two of them been laughing at me yesterday?

I wanted to run out of the room.

He held up the phone toward me.

"Check out Wu's video."

But I didn't look at the screen. Instead, I looked at John's face. The anger in me grew and grew until it was bigger than the hurt and humiliation he had caused, bigger than my fear that I would never break the counter-spell. How had I ever liked him? He was horrible.

"You're just a . . . a . . . jerk," I whispered, gripping the end of the bed and feeling myself, and my voice, grow-ing stronger as I spoke. The words Riley used to describe someone who he thought was really, really mean popped into my head. "You're just a big poo-poo head!" John looked up from his phone and stared at me, his big bushy beast eyebrows furrowed into an expression of shock and then disgust. I stepped closer to him and leaned in, point-ing my finger at his hairy face. "You deserve to look like that. You're ugly on the inside and the outside. You're a monster."

I turned around and almost bumped into his dad, who was walking into the room. As I ran to the elevators, I heard his dad gasp, but I didn't turn around.

In the elevator—a normal, modern one—I held back tears. I'd seen John's true self, *and* I'd done nothing to break the spell. I was a failure.

On the ground floor, I stormed out of the hospital, hardly catching my breath until I reached Romy, who was sitting on a bench. I briefly wondered how she'd gotten herself out of the hospital after the whole fainting thing.

She jumped to her feet when she saw me.

"Did you do it?" she asked excitedly, but then her face fell as I got closer. "Are you okay, Cia?"

"No," I said, sitting down on the bench beside her.

"What happened?" she asked.

"What happened is that John Lee is a jerk. He's horrible." I tried to keep the shake out of my voice, but I couldn't.

"So, you didn't kiss him. . . ."

"No," I snapped, "I didn't kiss him. There is no way I'm kissing that guy. Ever."

"Okay," said Romy softly. "What did he do?"

I told her.

"Yeah, he is a jerk," agreed Romy when I'd finished. "He's horrible." It felt good to hear her say it. I started to feel a bit better.

We both sat in silence for a moment.

"So, I guess he's still a beast, then?" asked Romy.

"Yeah." I looked up at the hospital tower where John Lee's room was and wondered how long he'd be in there. The doctors would never figure out that they were dealing with magic, not a disease. What specialist would diagnose collateral spell damage? The tiniest part of me felt bad for John—I was worried about going to school bald; what would it be like to show up with horns and covered in hair?—but there was just no way I could kiss him now. Not after what he had said to me. Just the thought of speaking to him made me feel awful.

Romy's phone beeped. She ignored it, but then it beeped again and again and again. As she pulled it out and looked at it, I kept my eyes on a grackle that was pecking the ground a few feet away from where we sat. I hoped it was in my head, but I thought the bird was looking at me in a menacing way.

"Cia," said Romy excitedly, holding out her phone to

me. "Raul just sent a text. John's cured! He's not a beast anymore."

I grabbed Romy's phone and stared at the screen. There was a selfie of John and his dad taken in the hospital room I had just left. His dad looked like he'd been crying—but he was smiling. So, happy tears. John looked just like John. He'd shrunk back to his normal size, and there were no horns on his head, no excessive body hair, no clawlike hands or bulging muscles. He looked like the boy I'd had a crush on all year.

"What?" I gasped. "How did this happen?"

I scrolled up to read Raul's first text. It had been sent a few minutes ago, just after I'd left John's room.

"What did you do?" said Romy. "He was a beast, and then you saw him, and then he wasn't a beast. What did you do?"

The same question was ricocheting around in my head. I turned to Romy and took off my baseball cap.

"How's my hair?" I asked. I lowered my head so that Romy had a clear view of the back.

"You've still got a bald patch," said Romy, standing on her tippy-toes. "It might even be a bit bigger than last time we checked. I don't get it. If John's not a beast anymore . . . doesn't that mean that the spell's been broken?"

"No," I said, sitting back down on the bench. "That's not how this thing works." I almost laughed. How had I not seen how it would play out? It was so obvious now. It was my liking John that had caused him to turn into a beast; so, when I stopped liking him, he stopped being a beast.

As soon as I fell out of like, the spell's hold over John was broken. Those few minutes with him in the hospital room had obliterated my crush and had obliterated the spell's effect on him.

I explained all this to Romy.

"So, the spell's not affecting John anymore," she clarified. "But it's still not broken?"

I nodded.

And, I realized, as long as the spell was still active, *any* boy I liked would be transformed into a beast. Maybe I'd have to become a nun, join an enclosed order where I wouldn't see anyone but the other nuns. But I didn't want to become a nun—for me, that felt like a worse fate than being bald and sleepless. I'd have to find some other way to avoid boys and keep any monster-making emotions under control. Though after what had just happened in John's hospital room, I couldn't imagine liking any boy ever again. I regretted every moment I had spent daydreaming about John Lee.

"Let's go back to Madame Fredepia," I said, feeling a sudden surge of energy. "The spell's not broken, but . . . the bit that was affecting John *is* broken." I had done *something*— not deliberately, but I had done something that had changed the magic. Maybe I was getting closer to breaking the spell completely. "If we fill her in on all the stuff that's happened today, maybe she'll actually help me. . . ." Madame Fredepia had said, *You have to help yourself*, and I'd done that. Sort of. Maybe she just wanted to see if I could help myself—like a test—and once I'd done that, she'd actually help me.

"I'll let Noah know we're ready to go," said Romy, taking back her phone.

I stood up and stamped my feet at the grackle. I didn't want any birds close to me. Ever again.

Within a few minutes, Noah pulled the car up to the curb, and we got in the back.

"Where to now, ladies?" said the nicest big brother in the world.

"Yo-Yo Swirl, please," said Romy.

"Ah, going for some double chocolate fudge delights?" said Noah.

Yeah, I thought, surprised at how optimistic I felt. *We will treat ourselves to some yogurt. Just as soon as Madame Fredepia tells me how to break the spell.*

Chapter 14

WHEN NOAH DROPPED US OFF AND ROMY and I ran to Madame Fredepia's, we found that the door was locked and that every square inch of it was plastered with NOTICE OF CESSATION OF BUSINESS signs. I pulled one off and read it.

THIS NOTICE HEREBY REVOKES MADAME FREDEPIA'S LICENSE TO PRACTICE MAGIC IN ANY OF THE FIFTY STATES OF AMERICA OR ITS TERRITORIES, SOUTH AMERICA, EUROPE, AFRICA, AUSTRALIA, ANTARTICA, ASIA, MEXICO, AND CANADA, AND

ALL OTHER REGIONS AS YET UNKNOWN TO THE
NON-MAGICAL COMMUNITY.

MADAME FREDEPIA IS CHARGED WITH THE FOLLOWING:

- FAILING TO CONSULT WITH HER SUPERIORS BEFORE
  ADMINISTERING UNTESTED SPELLS.
- THE IRRESPONSIBLE AND DESTRUCTIVE USE OF MAGIC.
- INTERFERING WITH THE PURSUIT OF THE HAPPILY
  EVER AFTER.

BY ORDER OF THE LEAGUE OF FAIRY GODMOTHERS

There was a red, waxy, official-looking stamp at the
end of the page, with a carving of a wand shooting out
stars embossed into it.

"What the . . . ?" Romy said under her breath.

So *that* was what LFGM meant. No wonder I couldn't
find anything when I'd googled it. At this point, I wasn't
even shocked that fairy godmothers existed. All I felt was
really disappointed that Madame Fredepia was gone. I'd
been so sure that now that I'd broken the spell's effect on
John, she'd help me. But this was a big dead end.

"Has she been arrested?" I asked, lifting one of the notices covering the window to try to peer into the building. But it was completely dark inside.

"I wouldn't say so," said Romy. "This is from the League of Fairy Godmothers. They don't sound like they'd arrest people."

"Do you really think Madame Fredepia's a fairy godmother?" I wondered. She hadn't said anything about granting wishes—wasn't that what they did?—and I couldn't imagine fairy godmothers smoking cigarettes like Madame Fredepia. "She didn't seem like one—"

"Didn't seem like a fairy godmother?" interrupted Romy, a note of anger in her voice. "Why are you so surprised that Madame Fredepia's a fairy godmother?" she continued, narrowing her eyes at me. "Because she's Black?"

"No, I—"

"You think because she's Black, she can't be a fairy godmother," said Romy accusingly, eyes flashing and hands on her hips.

I hadn't seen her this mad since her parents had confiscated her phone for a week when they'd realized she'd been up all night texting me.

"You were so shocked when you read that. I saw your face," continued Romy. She seemed to be getting madder and madder. "You don't think a Black woman can be a fairy godmother!"

"Romy, c'mon," I began. I was about to say that she was wrong and that of course I thought a fairy godmother could be Black! If I had looked shocked, it was because I was shocked that fairy godmothers were *real*, but was that what I really thought? Was Romy right? When I thought of a fairy godmother, the first thing that popped into my head was the white, chubby, gray-haired lady from the Disney Cinderella movies. I'd never seen a Black fairy godmother, so did that mean that I'd just assumed that fairy godmothers couldn't be Black? I felt my heart lurch and my face get red. I had made a horrible assumption. Just because I'd never seen anything other than a white fairy godmother, my brain had somehow decided that all fairy godmothers had to be white.

"I'm sorry, Romy," I said. "I think . . . I mean . . . you're right. . . . I never really thought about it. . . ."

"Yeah, people just don't think," she said, stuffing her hands into her pockets and staring at the ground.

She was fighting back tears. There was something

more going on here than my reaction to the news that Madame Fredepia was a fairy godmother. I stayed quiet, waiting for her to tell me if she wanted to.

"I got a text while you were in the hospital. From Mia. She wanted to know what role I'd tried out for in the spring play. I told her Juliet. And then she said . . ." Romy's voice cracked. "She texted, 'Are you sure you're right for that part?'"

"Romy . . ."

"I know what she meant, Cia. She meant I don't look right for that role. I'm too brown to be Juliet. I don't look the way Juliet is supposed to look."

She sat down on the curb and started to cry.

I sat down beside her, close enough so that our shoulders were touching, and put my hand on her arm. I felt so bad for Romy. Other people's comments could really hurt sometimes; I knew what that felt like. How someone's words could make you question yourself, doubt what you thought you were.

"You're awesome at acting, Romy, and you would be the best Juliet the school has ever had. Mia knows that. She's just . . . jealous."

"I'm okay," she said, wiping the tears and a little bit

of snot off her face with the back of her hand.

"You know Gavin wants to be Romeo," I said, trying to find something that would make Romy laugh. "He'd just about lose his mind if you were Juliet. He'd make you practice the balcony scene all day. . . . You'd never get away from him."

Romy smiled a tiny smile. Everyone in our class knew that Gavin had been crushing on her since fifth grade.

"What does all that mean anyway?" she said, pointing at the paper I had pulled off the locked door.

I looked down and reread the paper. "Madame Fredepia has been kicked out of the league for 'administering untested spells' and for 'the irresponsible and destructive use of magic.'"

"That sounds about right," said Romy. "So, do you think we could find anyone else in this league? Bet they'd know how to break the spell. . . ."

I agreed with Romy. The League of Fairy Godmothers had shut down Madame Fredepia for the "destructive use of magic," so wouldn't they want to help me, the victim of the destructive use of magic? I turned the notice over, but there was no extra information about where or how I could find other fairy godmothers.

Feeling totally deflated, I said, "There's no way to find them. I'm doomed." I crumpled the paper and tossed it in the big trash can on the curb. There were plenty more if we needed another copy.

I hadn't seen anything about a League of Fairy Godmothers in Mom's books or in the stuff in the attic. Would Mom have heard of them? I realized, annoyed with myself, that I should have called her back when I'd had the chance. She'd be on her flight from Australia now and would be home tomorrow night. I just had to get through tonight and tomorrow. I sighed loudly.

"What is it?" asked Romy.

"I'm just going to go home and wait this out," I said, thinking that I might skip school too. Bad things happened to me there. I might be safer at home. "Mom'll be back tomorrow night. She has to know how to fix this. I don't know what else I'm supposed to do. . . ."

"Want me to come sleep over?" asked Romy.

"Aw, thanks, Romy," I said, feeling my heart swell with gratitude for my friend. "It's okay. You've done so much already. Maybe when all this is over . . ." I really wanted

Romy to come back to my house, but I was worried that hanging out with me might be dangerous. Look what had happened to John. The magic from my spell had put him in the hospital. What might it do to my best friend? I didn't think best friends featured in the princess fairy tales—maybe that's why Cinderella and the rest of them were so helpless; they didn't have someone like Romy supporting them—but I couldn't be too careful. I didn't want anything bad to happen to Romy, ever.

"Well, text me if you change your mind," said Romy, raising a hand to wave at Noah, who was standing by his car in the parking lot. "Let's get out of here."

When I walked into the kitchen, I found Dad and Riley sitting at the counter. Riley's eyes were red and swollen as if he'd been crying.

"Ri," I said, dropping my backpack on the floor and running over to him. "What's wrong? What happened?" My mind started racing. Was there a fairy tale involving a princess's little brother? Was the spell—my spell—affecting Riley in some terrible way, the way it had affected John Lee?

"I can't do it," he said, his eyes filling up with tears.

I looked at Dad.

"The swimming lesson didn't go so well. Riley wouldn't put his head under the water."

I felt myself sag with relief. My spell wasn't affecting Riley. This was normal six-year-old stuff.

"I don't like it," said Riley. "I don't want to do it. I'm not brave. It's too scary."

"It's okay, Riley," I said, sitting down beside him. "It is kind of scary. I didn't like doing it either when I was learning to swim." He stared up at me, hanging on to every word I was saying, which made my heart fill up with love for him, but also made me hesitate. What if I said the wrong thing? What was the right thing to say? I thought about the *Do One Thing Every Day That Scares You* journal Mom had given me. Had I read something in there that would help Riley? "'Sometimes we just have to do the thing that scares us,'" I quoted, hating myself a bit because I couldn't stand that journal. "Being brave . . . That just means doing something even though it scares you."

Riley kept sniffling, but the tears slowed. It seemed like the words were helping. Maybe that journal wasn't completely awful.

"And the scary feeling—it just goes away when you start doing the scary thing, and then you realize that you're brave," I added, finding my own words. I'd been scared about visiting John Lee, and then I was actually able to figure things out—how to get into a restricted area and even find the words to tell him off when he was so horrible. I realized that maybe I had been a little brave myself today.

"Will you watch Captain Underpants with me?" asked Riley, his smile coming back.

"Sure," I said. "Do you think he swims with his cape on?"

Watching cartoons with Riley felt really good and normal, but once Riley and Dad went to bed and the house got quiet, all my worries came back. I called Mom's phone again even though I knew it was pointless. I just wanted to hear her voice on the voicemail message.

My heart began pounding when I saw notifications for four unread texts from John Lee. I swiped delete on the message thread, not wanting to hear another word from him or think about how much I used to like him. In addition to John's texts, there were almost a hundred messages from classmates about John's miraculous recovery. He'd been released from the hospital and had sent photos to the group of him being reunited with his dog. It was a really beautiful golden retriever, and John looked—at least from the photos—like he loved that dog. I still thought he was a jerk, but I had calmed down since the hospital visit and was relieved that John was not going to live out his life as a beast. No one deserved that. I realized too that if John had remained a beast, I would have had to live with that guilt forever. And that would have been awful.

I almost sent Mia a text telling her she should apologize to Romy for what she'd said, but how could I do that, when I'd sort of done the same thing? And Mia wasn't mean; she just said hurtful things sometimes. Like me. I texted Romy that she'd make an amazing Juliet. I didn't know what else to say, but I felt like there was something else I should be saying. Romy was my best friend. I thought we talked about everything, but we had never talked about this before, how having dark skin made things different for her.

I walked around the house, checking my hair in every mirror, but the bald patch didn't seem to have gotten any bigger. I almost wished all my hair would just fall out now so I could be done with dreading it happening. I was staring at my reflection in a mirror in my and Riley's bathroom, thinking about everything that happened in the past two days, when the sound of water running snapped me out of my thoughts.

I looked at the bathtub and saw that the water was filled to the very top, lapping over the edges and splashing out onto the tile. There were two containers of salt by the tub, and I realized—with horror—that I was holding a third in my hand.

I dropped it as if it were red-hot. I had no memory of filling up the tub. No memory of going downstairs and getting the salt. Why could I not remember, and why did I feel like I'd just narrowly avoided something terrible?

After turning off the faucet and throwing away all the salt in the house, I realized that I couldn't stay home alone tomorrow and just wait for Mom. It seemed that the spell had put me in a trance so that I had had no control over what I was doing. What if that happened again? I couldn't take the chance. I needed to be around people. I had to go to school.

Chapter 15

THE NEXT MORNING, THE WALK FROM THE school entrance to my locker was awful. I'd never been the center of attention before, and, as it turned out, I didn't like it. At. All.

I got stopped every few feet by a different person or group who wanted to high-five me or ask me questions about what was being referred to as the Attack of the Pigeons. An eighth grader, who was either a budding ornithologist or a full-blown conspiracy theorist, approached me to ask if I thought the birds had been controlled from a remote location.

After escaping the hallway, I met Romy in the restroom just as the bell was ringing for our first-period electives. I had chosen choir this semester, even though I wasn't much of a singer. Like everyone else in my family, I had no musical ability. But the only other available elective was the home economics class that Romy was heading to. Mr. Wilder, who taught it, acted like we should be preparing for life on a homestead in the 1880s. He taught things like baking, quilting, canning, and how to make candles from goat milk, and also blacksmithing, welding, and foraging. Last week, Romy had hand-spun Mr. Wilder's dog's hair into a bracelet, which just confirmed that I'd made the right choice with choir.

My plan for the day was to keep my head down and just hope that I'd make it to the end of the day without anything fairy tale–related happening. After looking under the doors to make sure no one else was in the restroom, I filled Romy in on my close call with the tub and salt, and she said she'd meet me after every class to make sure I hadn't fallen into a trance.

Mrs. Stasevich taught choir. During our first class at the beginning of the semester, she told us that she used to be an opera singer in Russia. The way she described it, people loved her so much that she couldn't walk across the stage because of all the roses adoring fans kept flinging at her feet. I was pretty sure teaching a group of middle schoolers to sing was not what she'd hoped she'd be doing after performing at the Moscow Conservatory. We'd only had a few weeks of choir so far, and she'd already kicked out two kids because she said their voices made her want to vomit.

We'd been practicing a choral round for the past few classes, with the choir divided into groups of three and each group starting the same song at different times. The idea was that all our voices would eventually come together in unison to sing the melody. Emphasis on *idea*, because we couldn't seem to make it happen. We ended up off-key and out of sync. Which didn't bother me. I claimed my usual spot at the edge of the room, ready to mumble through the class.

Mrs. Stasevich sighed wearily and pointed her baton at my group, and we began to sing. She walked toward the piano and suddenly stopped, pivoted on her heels, and turned around to face us. She raised her left hand and gripped her baton in the other so tightly that her knuckles whitened.

"Again," she said. "Sing that again."

She closed her eyes and came closer to us, stopping in front of me and standing so close that I could see her nostrils twitching. She was sniffing like a dog that had caught a whiff of something interesting.

"You!" she shouted. I jumped from the shock of being yelled at and the way Mrs. Stasevich's piercing eyes were staring at me. "It is you." She tapped her baton on my shoulder. "Step forward."

I stepped away from the others, bracing myself. It would be soap-making and hemming with Mr. Wilder from now on for me.

"No one else sing." She glared at the choir. "Not a squeak."

She tapped me on my lower back with her baton.

"Now you, stand straight, shoulders back, chest out." She walked over to her piano. "Sing what I play."

The melody started in the middle keys and ended with the highest note on the piano. I'd never heard the tune before, but I repeated the notes. I heard my classmates gasp behind me.

My voice was beautiful. It was astonishingly beautiful.

Mrs. Stasevich kept playing and I kept singing. It was glorious. I could sing! I felt like this was what I had been born to do. I instinctively lifted up my head and threw out my arms, all the better to expand the vocal cords and let the music flow out of me. At some point, Mrs. Stasevich started singing with me, pushing my voice to new heights so that it seemed like nothing existed other than the amazing sounds that I was making. When we finished singing, my classmates clapped and roared and whooped and hugged me. Tears were streaming down Mrs. Stasevich's face. I felt like a star.

Then I remembered. "The Little Mermaid."

If my singing had made Mrs. Stasevich gasp that I sounded like the love child of Freddie Mercury and Maria Callas (whoever they were) and brought the tech theater class from the room next door running in with their mouths hanging open, it could only mean one thing.

The counterspell.

Without asking for permission, I ran out of the class and headed for the closest restroom. As I raced down the hall, I heard Mrs. Stasevich's booming voice addressing my classmates. "Let her go. She is an artist. She needs to be alone. The artist pays a great price. . . ."

Oh, you have no idea, Mrs. Stasevich, I thought as I jogged down the stairs. Romy burst into the stairway and was right on my heels. I guess my voice and the applause had carried all the way to the home economics room. I was dimly aware of heads popping out of doors as we sped by.

Once in the restroom, Romy stood with her back to the door, keeping it shut.

"My legs?" I gasped.

"You've still got 'em." Romy pointed tentatively. Her hands were covered with blue ink. She'd obviously run out of Mr. Wilder's room mid-craft.

I jumped up and down, swiveled my legs side to side, bent my knees, and kicked furiously. If I kept moving my legs, just kept using them, then maybe I'd be able to keep them.

"But for how much longer?" I asked. "How much longer will I be able to do this?" I skipped across the restroom floor. "And this?" I hopped on one foot and then the other. "All of a sudden I can sing? I couldn't sing yesterday, and today I'm the next winner of *The Voice*. The Little Mermaid gave away her voice, and she got legs. Now I've got the voice, so I'm going to have to give away my legs."

"Maybe not," said Romy.

"What do you mean?" I gulped. "That's how this one works. Legs for a voice. That's how the counterspell works."

"Well, maybe this is just it," said Romy. "This is all there is to that part of the spell. The little-mermaid part of the spell. You just get her great singing voice."

"And keep my legs?" I asked, grabbing on to them as if they were about to disappear.

"Maybe?" said Romy.

Romy was always looking at the world with her rose-tinted glasses and focusing on the best possible scenario, but could she be right? Maybe I wouldn't have to become a mermaid. I'd make a terrible mermaid. I wouldn't have long, flowing hair, or even my normal shoulder-length hair. The other mermaids would make fun of me. I'd be a mermaid outcast!

"Okay," I said, desperately wanting to be as optimistic as Romy. "I'm going to keep my legs."

Romy turned on a faucet and started washing her hands. I stared at the gushing water, feeling a pull toward it.

"Turn it off!" I squealed.

"What?" asked Romy, looking at me in the mirror.

"Water," I said. "I need to stay away from water." I remembered how awful I had felt last night when I'd seen the tub of water, the sense of dread that had come over me. Now I realized that if I hadn't snapped out of that trance, I would have stepped into that bath, and it would have been the last time I stepped anywhere. I felt sure of it.

I needed to stay away from water. And, to be on the safe side, to never sing again.

I could do that, right? If I did those two things, then maybe—just maybe—I could postpone my mermaid destiny until I figured out how to break the spell. The second part would involve incurring the wrath of Mrs. Stasevich, but I could handle her. The first part, though, the not washing, was potentially disgusting and socially catastrophic.

"I'm going home," I announced.

"You're just going to skip school?" said Romy, looking shocked.

"I've gotta get out of here, Romy." Before Mrs. Stasevich showed up and asked me to sing again.

Leaving Romy still standing by the sink, I ran down the hallway and straight past Mrs. Brennan's desk.

"I've gotta go," I said, opening the front doors.

She could write me up, put me in detention, even expel me. I really didn't care. I had a lot more at stake than maintaining my perfect school attendance record.

I ran toward the bike stand, noticing that there was a large orange beanbag in the middle of all the bikes. Why had someone left that there? As I got closer, I realized that it wasn't a beanbag. It was an enormous pumpkin.

I didn't even have to look for my bike amidst all the others to know what had happened. Lying on top of the pumpkin was my bright blue bicycle lock. The pumpkin was my bike. My bike had been turned into a pumpkin.

"Oh, c'mon!" I glanced around me to see if there was a fairy godmother peering over the shrubbery (was this their idea of a joke?) or a few talkative mice scampering around. There was nothing.

I stared at the pumpkin. It came up to my waist. I could add "Owner of World's Largest Squash" to my record-breaking list.

I patted my bike/pumpkin goodbye and started walking.

Chapter 16

I TOOK THE ROUTE HOME THAT CUT THROUGH Mallory Park. It had a playground and just enough green space for an outdoor yoga group and some kind of Mommy and Me music class. I resisted the urge to run up to the mothers and warn them not to ruin their babies' lives by taking them to fairy godmothers masquerading as fortune-tellers/baby-whisperers.

My mind was racing as I walked. The bike-to-pumpkin transformation had to be another side effect of the counterspell. My "carriage" had been turned into a large vegetable. I realized in the grand scheme of things that losing my bike wasn't a big deal, but it made me mad.

A cute little girl wearing a sparkly dress and a tiara on her head cut across my path. I thought about what Mom had said to Madame Fredepia about not wanting me to buy into any of "that princess nonsense." Would wearing a tiara and frilly outfit now mean that this little girl would grow up and think that she had to look and act a certain way to get a "prince"? But it wasn't even like Mom's decision to take me to Madame Fredepia had helped me to avoid all the princess nonsense—it had ended up turning me into a damsel in distress. The very thing Mom had wanted to avoid! I'd love if a prince showed up now and rescued me. I'd happily stick a tiara on my head if it would attract a rescuing prince, or anyone, really, to save me from this nightmare of a fairy tale.

I pulled out my phone and called Mom. As I expected, it went straight to voicemail, but I still left a message.

"Mom, you need to call me back NOW. Remember Madame Fredepia? Terrible things are happening. You need to call me."

I picked up my pace and reached the other side of the park. Back on the main street, I noticed for the first time that every other store I passed seemed to be in the business of making women "beautiful." There was a lash bar where you could get eyelash extensions, a tanning salon for "that sun-kissed glow," hair salons offering straight hair or curly hair, nail salons with dazzling displays of polishes, weight loss clinics, beauty stores with exotic-sounding brands and sleek interiors. And inside every one, there were women buying into it all. Literally—the signs advertising the services told me that this stuff wasn't cheap.

I stopped in front of the window of a bridal shop that displayed magnificent creations of tulle and lace and beads. The words "Live the Fairy Tale" were written in beautiful calligraphic script across the window.

How had I never seen this before?

Was Mom right? Was this pressure to be a "princess" really everywhere? Was she right to complain about how skin care companies advertised, and how princesses destroyed girls' self-esteem? I thought about Romy and how sad and mad she had been the day before because Mia had thought she wasn't "right" for the Juliet role. Why had Mia said that? I started thinking about the movies I'd seen of Cinderella, Snow White, Sleeping Beauty, Belle, the

Little Mermaid. They were the princesses that everyone seemed to know about. They were the important ones. The ones with the dolls that looked like them and the costumes and the lunch boxes and pretty much anything else that you could put their pictures on. And they were all white. They were always white.

How had I never noticed that before?

And how did all this make Romy feel? The only super-popular princess that looked a bit like her was Jasmine from "Aladdin." But that was just one Disney princess. My mind started jumping around, thinking about all the others. There was Mulan and Tiana and Pocahontas and Moana. But that was just five out of how many? Fifteen? Once all this was over, when I had gotten rid of this awful spell, I was going to ask Romy how she felt about it all.

Just as I got to my house, my phone beeped. It was a message from Romy.

I'm coming over. You might zone out and run a bath or something.

I started typing in a message telling her not to come, but then I realized that Romy was going to come over no matter what I said. I deleted my message.

I opened the front door and heard the TV, even

though no one was home. Dad must have left it on. I went into the living room to turn it off, but I stood mesmerized when I saw what was on it. A news channel was reporting on what was called—according to the news ticker at the bottom of the screen—"Birthday Party Princess Turns Violent." There was footage that looked like it was from someone's phone of a family's encounter with Cinderella at a birthday party. Cinderella was greeting a delighted little girl and a sulky older boy who didn't look up from his ice cream when Cinderella spoke to him. In response, Cinderella grabbed the cone and rammed the chocolate twist with rainbow sprinkles into the boy's forehead. The mother yelled at Cinderella, who kicked the woman in the shins, lifted up her ball gown, and ran. As far as I could see, both shoes stayed on. The footage ended, and it switched to the news anchor talking in the studio where a legal expert weighed in on the assault charges and lawsuit for emotional distress that the family was bringing.

A mug shot of Cinderella popped up on the screen, her sparkly tiara slightly askew, and she was staring into the camera with a look of anger and disgust. The news anchor said that someone had posted bail of ten thousand dollars for Cindy Graff and that she had been fired from her job at Princess Parties, the service that provided—according to the news anchor—"magical birthday memories." Cindy Graff, the anchor continued, was countersuing her old employer for wrongful dismissal.

This was bizarre. There was something hilarious, yet terribly wrong, about seeing a mug shot of a fairy-tale princess. How often did a princess assault a guest at a birthday party? Had this happened before, or was this the first time, and if it was the first time, wasn't the timing a bit strange? Just as I was dealing with fairy-tale-related chaos, a princess-for-hire lost control—and how weird was it that her real name was Cindy? Almost as if . . .

My phone rang in my back pocket, startling me. I checked the number. I felt a lump in my throat and tears stinging my eyes.

"Mom!"

"Cia! Cia, sweetheart, what is going on?"

It was so good to hear her voice. I didn't know how to begin.

"Mom," I said, "I . . ."

Then the doorbell rang.

"Mom, can you hold on a second? Romy's at the door."

But it wasn't Romy.

When I opened the door, there was a giant woman, dressed in a white T-shirt and pants, standing in front of me. My eyes were level with her enormous chest, on which was emblazoned SHINY. She was carrying a broom and a bucket filled to the brim with bottles of bleach and Windex.

"We're here to clean," she said. She had an accent. The *w* sounded like a *v*. "Your fazzer called us."

Dad liked to call in cleaning services when Mom was out of town. Mom felt the same way about using a cleaning service as she did about buying flowers on Valentine's Day—both were a waste of money. But Dad thought doing housework was mind-numbingly boring and a waste of time. So, when Mom was gone, he did things his way.

"Oh, okay," I said. The woman looked over her shoulder and let out a long whistle.

I stepped back to let her in, putting the phone back to my ear, but I lost my words again as I watched what happened next. The rest of the crew that walked through the front door were all as big as Shiny. They all carried mops or vacuum cleaners and wore the same white T-shirt with a name stretched across the front. I read each T-shirt as each lady passed me. There was a BRIGHTLY, a TIDY, a NEATLY, and a GLEAMING. By the time I read SPECKLESS, I realized who they were. I counted them just to be sure.

Yup, there were seven. The seven dwarfs, now super-sized cleaning ladies, were in my house. And judging by the vigor with which they were beginning to attack the dirt—Sparkly was on her hands and knees scrubbing the grooves in between the kitchen tiles with a toothbrush—they were nothing like the slovenly, messy gang Snow White had moved in with.

"Mom," I gasped into the phone. "You're not going to believe this. . . ."

Then I felt my knees buckle as I was kicked from behind. Before I could tell Mom what was happening, I dropped my phone, and it went flying across the floor, skidding to a stop under the couch and completely out of reach. All seven cleaning ladies/giants/dwarfs came over to where I had fallen onto the runner in the hallway, and they lifted up the rug and rolled it around me like I was the sausage in a sausage roll. Then they hoisted me up on their shoulders and walked out the front door.

I tried to squirm and kick, but it was pointless; the rug was tucked in so tightly around me. Only my head was free. I shouted for help, but Shiny placed a big calloused palm over my mouth. I swiveled my head to the side and saw where they were taking me. The back doors of a white van were wide open, ready to receive me. There were words written along the side of the van, and if I hadn't been so terrified, I would have laughed.

SNOW WHITE CLEANING SERVICE.

Chapter 17

AFTER THEY PUT ME IN THE BACK OF THE VAN AND
Shiny removed her hand from my mouth, I used the
opportunity to scream my head off, yelling, "HELP!"
as we sped along to wherever it was they were taking me.
I tried to wiggle my way out of the rug I was wrapped in,
but all I did was make myself sweatier and more uncomfortable. Breathing heavily, I took in my surroundings.
From where I was on the floor of the van, I couldn't see
anything other than the cleaning supplies that rolled by my
head whenever the van made a sharp turn. We were moving so fast I wondered if there was an eighth dwarf called

Speedy in the driver's seat. I hardly had time to beat myself up for not remembering all the "STRANGER DANGER!" lectures from elementary school when the van screeched to a halt and the back doors opened.

I was hoisted up on shoulders again and marched into, as I expected, a cottage-style house. The giant women moved too quickly for me to take in the neighborhood, so I wasn't able to tell if I'd traveled out into the countryside or if I was still in the suburban sprawl that surrounded my house. All I could see as I moved through the cottage was the ceiling. The women came to a stop and unrolled the rug, and I fell out of it onto the floor.

"What is going on?" I shouted, coughing and spitting bits of carpet fibers out of my mouth. I tried to get up, but a wave of dizziness hit me.

A woman looked down at me, but she wasn't one of the cleaners. Instead, she was picture-book perfect. Jet-black hair in a swishy ponytail, peachy skin, rosebud lips, dark blue—almost black—eyes framed with impossibly long eyelashes. Straight out of the Brothers Grimm's book.

It was Snow White.

I pushed myself up off the floor so that I was standing.

The panic I'd been feeling subsided a bit. Snow White was here. Snow White was sweet and nice. This was good news, wasn't it?

She walked away without offering to help or saying a word, which I thought was very unprincessy of her. She sat down on a chair in the corner of the room and stared at me. A furry brown creature scampered up her leg and sat on her lap, where she petted it like it was a cat. It was a squirrel. It looked exactly like the squirrel that had stolen my chips the previous day, but I couldn't be sure.

I considered making a quick curtsy or bow (wasn't she royalty?) but reconsidered when I saw the way she was looking at me, regarding me as if I were a piece of gum she had just found at the bottom of her very dainty shoe. She might have been beautiful, but she didn't look like a nice person. Rather, she looked like someone who would mastermind a kidnapping. Is that what had just happened? Had I just been kidnapped by Snow White?

"What is going on?" I repeated, looking around for the nearest exit. The only door I saw seemed to lead into a bedroom. I could see a row of bunk beds on the other side of the door.

Snow White crossed her legs and pointed a slippered foot at a high-backed yellow chair.

"Do sit down," she said. She spoke suspiciously sweetly in a way that reminded me of my old third-grade teacher who didn't raise her voice once the entire year and then, on the last day of school, took off her shoe and threw it at Hudson Bayer for picking his nose.

"I want to go home right now," I said, still standing. I hoped I sounded braver than I felt. I looked around for Shiny and the others, but there was no one in the room other than me and Snow White.

Despite the bad vibes I was getting from Snow White, I had to admit, it was a very nice room. It had high ceilings crisscrossed with big wooden rafters, and a stone floor covered with colorful rugs that were much nicer than the one I had rolled in on. The walls were covered with book-shelves, and one of the walls was decorated with mirrors, paintings, and picture frames. The paintings and pic-tures were so big that I was able to see the images in them clearly from where I stood in the middle of the room, and I realized they were all of brides and grooms, getting progressively more modern from one end of the wall to the other. The display of art was bookended on one side with a huge oil painting, like something you'd see in a museum, with a man and a woman wearing lots of velvet and jewels, and on the other side with a photo of a woman in a white, lacy dress cutting a cake, a tuxedoed man standing next to her. In between there were more paintings of brides and grooms followed by photos of brides and grooms. All the brides were young and dark-haired and beautiful, but the men got older and more miserable looking and generally less attractive as you worked your way across the wall. In looking around, I realized with a sinking feeling that there were no windows—meaning fewer options for escape.

"You can't just go around kidnapping people," I continued, wondering if I should just turn and run, but I wasn't sure which way to go. When you've entered a room inside a rug, it's difficult to get your bearings.

"Kidnapping is nothing compared with what you've done," said Snow White, a hint of steel in her sweet voice.

"I haven't done anything!" I said. She was the one who had kidnapped me!

"You are messing with my happily ever after," said

Snow White, smoothing out her dress. "I've had five cancellations this week."

What was she talking about? Running a cleaning service and employing a gang of criminal women wasn't even what Snow White was supposed to be doing. Wasn't she supposed to be living in a castle with a prince? And wasn't that supposed to be happening in a fairy-tale world or in whatever parallel universe those stories played out, not in Brooklyn within a few miles from my house? And what did any of that have to do with me?

If Snow White and her dwarfs were here—not to mention the fairy godmothers that were flying around posting notices—and possibly turning things (my bike) into vegetables, did that mean that other fairy-tale characters were here too? Like Cindy from the afternoon news? What did it mean if fairy-tale characters were actually real and living here among us?

My heart was hammering hard, pumping blood at such a furious rate that I felt light-headed. But I refused to sit down, because that was what Snow White wanted me to do. I took a deep breath and counted to ten, the way Riley, who'd learned it from his soccer coach, had shown me.

I needed to back up and get some facts.

"So, hold on a minute," I began. "You're Snow White. THE Snow White?"

"Yes."

"And you live here . . . ?"

"Of course I live here," snapped Snow White. "This is where the stories happen." She stomped a foot on the ground. "The happily ever after happens here."

"Okay," I said, pausing to choose my words carefully, feeling like a member of a bomb squad figuring out which wire to cut. Snow White looked like she might lose her temper easily. I decided to ask about something that wasn't likely to upset her. "So, are you waiting for your prince to come?"

"Waiting doesn't work anymore." She pouted. "We haven't done that for about thirty years. The men have gotten too lazy. There was a time they'd seek us out. Liked nothing more than a good quest." She pointed at the gallery of wedding pictures. The guys in the older paintings were on horses, carrying swords, and looked like they'd be well able for a bit of questing, but most of the guys in the newer photographs looked like they wouldn't be able to even get up on a horse. "These days you have to prac-tically throw yourselves in front of them to get noticed." She sat up straighter, bristling with irritation. "And no one's come close to marrying an actual prince for *decades*. Not this side of the world anyway. Belle's in Paris. And they've got some actual royalty over there. It's Europe, you know? But Belle doesn't try hard enough." She tut-ted disapprovingly. "And there's that Little Mermaid, who was about to marry a prince in Saudi Arabia—LM does best when there's a language barrier—until *you* started messing things up." She gave me a withering look. "We have to go out to find the princes now. And make it easy for them to find us. Rapunzel runs Shear Success, the hair salon for men." She paused.

I'd heard of it. Dad called it the "I'll Fleece You Hair Studio" because they charged two hundred dollars for a haircut.

"Well, it's very expensive," continued Snow White. "And Rapunzel just needs the right man to sit in one of her chairs. A few shampoos later, she'll get a marriage proposal out of him, and there's her happily ever after."

"And what about you?" I asked.

"Same principle as Rapunzel. Just wait for the right client. Shiny and the rest of the gang do the reconnaissance work. Pretty easy to find out how rich someone is when you're in his home." She reached into a pocket and pulled out some nuts and fed them to the squirrel. "Sylvester does a little investigative work too. . . ."

Had Sylvester been investigating me? Had he been the one who had pounced on me at school? I stared at his little face, and he stared back at me, making a chirruping noise that I assumed translated to *I've got your chips*. It *was* him.

"Once a target is identified," Snow White continued, "I show up and, well . . ."

She paused and flashed me a dazzlingly bright smile. She really was astonishingly beautiful.

"I don't like to brag, but I've been known to get a marriage proposal within twenty-four hours." Her gaze fell again on the gallery of pictures. I took a step closer to the wall and stared at them. How had I not noticed it earlier? It was the same bride in all the pictures. Snow White was in every single one of them.

How many times had she been married? There were hundreds of wedding photos on the wall. She was sitting here in her gorgeous home in Brooklyn running her cleaning/husband-hunting business, but what about all the guys she had married? Where were the men?

"What? What about the . . . you know . . . your husbands?" I gasped. I stared at Snow White, who was clearly not the sweet and gentle soul I had always thought she was. What had she done to all those men she'd married? Was her fairy tale actually a horror movie?

"Oh, they just go back to whatever they were doing before," she said matter-of-factly. "I get my happily ever after, and then I have to find another one."

What? *Find another one?* Why?

"But isn't that the whole point of 'happily ever after'?" I argued. "That it's forever after? You find your prince— or he finds you—and then you live happily ever after. You know . . . then that's the end of the story."

"No." Snow White tutted. "Don't you know anything about fairy tales? The story ends, and then it starts up again."

I stared at the gallery of pictures as Snow White's words sank in. If I was processing all of this right, she was stuck on a hamster wheel of marriage proposals and weddings. Didn't she get sick of it? Didn't she want it to stop? I thought about how Mom called the princesses "poor deluded fools"—is this what she was talking about? That all they wanted to do was to find their "princes" and have big weddings?

"But," I said, "what does any of this have to do with me?"

"You!" shouted Snow White. "You're messing things up! There's magic radiating off you." She wrinkled her nose as if I smelled of old eggs. "And it's affecting me and the other princesses."

"That's impossible! I don't have anything to do with magic," I pleaded. "A woman put a spell on me when I was a baby—that's it. Why would that affect you?"

But even as I said it, I knew the spell that was cast on me had affected John—it had turned him into a beast. And I had worried that it might affect other people like Romy and Riley. Was it possible that the counterspell was also affecting the very princesses whom it was designed to stop me from imitating? My heart dropped. It was possible. That was exactly how this spell seemed to play out. It turned everything upside down.

"But it's not my fault," I said. "And I've been trying to figure out how to break the spell ever since I found out about it."

"Well, you need to get it done. You need to break that spell," snapped Snow White, glaring at me. "The side effects are disastrous. My cleaning crew grew a couple of feet in one night. They can't fit into their beds anymore."

She pointed at the open doorway, and I looked again at the bunk beds. Shiny and the rest of them would have to sleep with their knees hanging over the edges of the beds. It would be uncomfortable, but I had a hard time feeling sorry for my kidnappers.

"And LM's in a terrible way. Her story says she can enchant the prince with"—Snow White paused and recited—"'lovely form, gliding movements, and eloquent eyes.'" She counted everything out on her fingers. "But," she said, glaring at me, "now she's tripping over her own feet and has developed a squint. That prince has run for the hills.

"Rapunzel's salon is falling apart. Shear Success has no water in the pipes, blunt scissors, and exploding hair dryers. Cinderella's gone off the rails. I told her not to take that job with the party planning place. None of us can handle that kind of pressure. But she failed the audition for a reality TV show—one of those where a single man has to pick his wife from twenty candidates. She's *never* lost one of those. So she took that princess party job as a last resort—and look how that turned out."

So, the shin-kicking Cindy at the birthday party was *the* Cinderella. The horror must have shown on my face.

"Cinderella is not happy with you," said Snow White. "She is very upset."

Something occurred to me.

"Did she send birds to my school?" I asked, feeling furious. I could have been blinded in that attack. My classmates could have been hurt. And poor Mrs. Taylor was scarred for life! Emotionally, that is. "Big mean pigeons?"

She shrugged. "Probably. Sounds like something Cinderella would do."

So Cinderella was as bad as Snow White. They were like a couple of crime bosses. "What about a deer?" I said, wanting to put all the pieces together, to see the whole picture. "Would she have sent a deer?"

"Wouldn't put it past her," said Snow White. "She's really into intimidation tactics."

These princesses were mean. These weren't the sweet, obliging, can't-stand-up-for-themselves girls I'd read about and seen in the movies. They were even worse. Cinderella sounded particularly dangerous. Admittedly, no one was all that perfect in the Brothers Grimm versions, but Disney made them practically angelic. Either Walt Disney had gotten his facts wrong, or the side effects of the counterspell were making the princesses devious and ruthless. Either way, this all meant that I didn't just have to figure out how to break the ridiculous counterspell—I had to worry about mean princesses, too.

"Just break the spell," snapped Snow White. "And we can all get back to doing what we're supposed to be doing."

"I can't," I said. "I want to. I really, really want to." And I did, desperately, though I couldn't help but think that Snow White and the rest of them could use a break from the happily-ever-after carousel they were spinning around on. But that wasn't my problem. "I just don't know how to do it."

Snow White pursed her lips together.

"But you," I said, seeing a possible way out. "Could you break it?"

"I can't break spells!" shouted Snow White, surprising me. "Who do you think I am? Princesses don't break spells."

"Well, neither do thirteen-year-old girls," I said, trying to sound lighthearted and friendly, hoping that having something in common would make her realize that we were on the same side.

It didn't. She looked like she wanted to hit me. I took a tiny step back.

"Such a shame," said Snow White. "I didn't want to have to do this. You remind me of a seamstress my stepmother had a long time ago."

She stood up.

"But . . ." She sighed impatiently. "If you can't do it, then there is no other way. If the spell cannot be broken, then the one in whom the spell lives must be destroyed."

Chapter 18

I WASN'T COMPLETELY CERTAIN, BUT I WAS pretty sure Snow White was threatening to kill me. *The one in whom the spell lives must be destroyed* had to be the worst words I had ever heard.

She stayed perfectly poised in her chair and just kept staring at me like she was waiting for me to make the first move. Where were the cleaning ladies? Wouldn't they be the ones doing the destroying . . . unless Snow White had a weapon hidden in her dress or something? I whirled around, looking for a way out, but still the only door I could see was the one behind Snow White into the bedroom. If that room had some windows, though, I could smash one open. I could yell for help.

I ran toward the open door, my arms in front of me, ready to shove Snow White out of the way if she launched herself out of the chair. But she didn't move. Right before reaching the door, I felt the ground open underneath me. I screamed as I fell down a hole, hitting my arms and legs against steps as I tumbled down. I grunted in pain when I landed on a stone floor.

Looking up, and hoping nothing was broken, I saw Snow White gazing down at me from the top of a flight of stairs. With a sinking feeling, I realized I had fallen through a trapdoor into a basement.

"You'll have to wait here," she shouted down at me. "Shiny and the others will take care of the mess when they come back. I don't want to break a nail." She waved a manicured hand at me. "Bye-bye, little girl."

She slammed the trapdoor shut, leaving me in darkness.

For a moment, I just sat on the ground thinking about the ways the cleaners might clean up the mess that was me. Would they force me to drink bleach? Spray Windex in my eyes? Crush me with their massive arms?

I shuddered and then winced. It hurt to move. I was pretty sure my thirteen-year, no-breaks-fractures-or-sprains streak had come to an end. The only serious injury I'd ever had was a playground concussion when I was ten, when I'd gotten a little bit too Cirque du Soleil on the monkey bars.

I stood up carefully, testing each limb for serious pain, and looked around me. My eyes were beginning to adjust to the gloom, and I could now see that the basement was about the size of my bedroom. There were shafts of daylight coming in through windows that were too small and too high up for me to climb out of. Other than some brooms and a couple of buckets in one of the corners, the space was empty. Not knowing what else to do or try, I walked back up the stairs and banged on the underside of the trapdoor.

"Let me out!" I yelled, even though I knew it was pointless.

I pushed the trapdoor with both hands. It didn't budge. I positioned my shoulders and rammed myself against it, grunting with the effort and the pain. Same result. It didn't move. It felt like it was nailed shut.

I returned to the bottom step and sat down, wondering how I could defend myself with a broom and a bucket. Even if I was some sort of martial arts expert—which I wasn't—I couldn't pull off a fight with seven bigger, meaner, musclier opponents. I couldn't outfight *anyone*. Was this it? Was I going to be finished off by a gang of supersized dwarfs? Mom had been so determined to keep me away from fairy-tale nonsense, and this was how it was all going to end?

Had Mom known about this? Not the out-to-get-me part, but the fact that fairy-tale princesses were real. Where, I wondered desperately, were the fairy-tale princes? I didn't care what Mom thought; at this point, I would have loved one to show up now and rescue me.

Suddenly the basement flooded with light.

"Visitors for you!" shouted Snow White from above.

I looked behind me and scrambled out of the way, narrowly missing a tumbling Romy, who landed beside me.

"Romy!" I hugged her. I was so happy to see her.

She was followed by John Lee, who, after he came to a tumbling stop, ran back up the steps and started yelling, pounding, and pushing on the trapdoor.

"That Snow White's not very nice," mumbled Romy.

"What are you doing here?" I asked.

"She's a homicidal maniac," said John, walking down the steps.

I laughed before remembering that I couldn't stand him. He looked way better than last time I'd seen him, like a normal seventh grader, which I was happy about, but I wasn't happy to see *him*.

"What's he doing here?" I asked Romy. "What are *you* doing here?"

"Well, John really wanted to talk to you, so when I said I was going to your house . . . he wanted to come too. And when we got there, the front door was wide open, so we walked in and figured out there was no one home, and then I found this on the kitchen counter."

She pulled a business card out of her pocket and handed it to me. SNOW WHITE CLEANING SERVICE was printed in large letters at the top.

"And I found your phone on the floor," she continued. "So I knew something was going on—you always have your phone." She pulled it out of her pocket and handed it to me. I checked it. There was no signal. I put it in the back pocket of my jeans.

"So," said Romy, "we decided to find the address on the card."

"Nice work, Nancy Drew," I said, feeling a flood of emotions—happy that she was here, but also sick to my stomach that now she was in danger too. I didn't see how having her and John here increased the chances of fighting off and escaping from the giant cleaning ladies. We were still way outnumbered. And outmuscled.

John was throwing sheepish looks in my direction, but I ignored him and looked at Romy. He held up his phone in front of him and walked around the basement as if he was trying to pick up a signal. I lowered my voice—I didn't feel like sharing everything that had just happened with John—and talked to Romy. I told her about the kidnapping and that the princesses were real, finishing with the most important detail, that the cleaning crew would soon be returning to kill me. And I figured that they'd have similar plans for Romy and John, too.

"I think it's going to be okay," said Romy.

I wondered if she had hit her head on the way down the stairs. In the first few moments after my playground concussion, I had thought I could speak French.

"How is it going to be okay?" I asked. "We're trapped in a basement with no way out. And when that trapdoor opens again, murderous dwarfs will be on the other side of it."

"You just need to kiss John," she said, lowering her voice.

"Not this again," I said. I swiveled my eyes in John's direction. He was sitting on the bottom step with his head in his hands. I couldn't see his face. I wondered how much Romy had told him about what was going on.

"You didn't do it last time," said Romy, her forehead and eyes creased into a frown. "There's always a kiss in those fairy-tale stories, Cia."

John cleared his throat, cutting through my thoughts.

"Cia," he said, leaning forward on his elbows and looking over at me. He stared at me for a fraction of a second and then looked at the ground. "I just want to say I'm sorry. I'm really sorry for the things I said to you yesterday. I don't know why I did that."

I felt the anger and embarrassment I had felt in the hospital room returning.

"I don't want to talk about it," I said, folding my arms. If I was going to be taken down by Snow White's dwarfs, I didn't want to spend my last few minutes listening to John Lee and thinking about that horrible hospital visit.

"Look," John continued, still gazing at the ground. "When I was sick, I felt really angry and really powerful. I just wanted to punch things and smash things and hurt people. I don't understand why. I can't really remember all of it . . . but I know I was a jerk. I was a jerk to you. I didn't mean those things I said." He glanced up at me and quickly looked back down. "And I needed to say sorry. And when you wouldn't reply to my texts, I went to your house to apologize."

He stopped looking at the ground and turned his head toward me.

"I'm really, really sorry. Just do whatever you need to do. . . ."

The light was dim, but I could see his face reddening before he looked back down at the ground. He had obviously figured out that the discussion Romy and I had been having had been about him. And kissing. I felt myself blush too and cringed with embarrassment.

"See," said Romy, standing up. "He's sorry. Now let's get this done before the dwarf assassins show up."

I nodded. John did seem really sorry. He had looked at me with the same regretful, puppy-eyed expression that Riley did when he'd confessed that he'd cracked the screen of my phone.

While I was ready to try anything at this point, I didn't believe kissing John was going to do anything other than embarrass him and me. It just didn't seem possible that a kiss would be enough to break a spell that had—among other things—eliminated my need to sleep, transformed me into a world-class singer, and given me the power to turn a boy into a beast. How could a kiss be big enough to wipe out that big of a spell?

But Romy believed that it was the way to go, and she had done so much for me, including joining me in a basement prison. Trying out her plan was the least I could do.

"Fine," I said. "I'll kiss him."

John got to his feet and stood up straight, with his shoulders thrown back, like a soldier reporting for duty. He looked so serious, like he was going to salute me. I almost laughed that this was how my first kiss was going to happen. But there was really nothing funny about being locked in a basement, terrified about a soon-to-happen attack, getting ready to kiss a boy who had just the day before as good as told you that you were ugly.

"You sure you're okay with this, John?" I asked, walking toward him. I was surprised at how I was feeling. I'd been so jittery and excited just before I went into his hospital room, when I'd been gearing myself up to ask him to kiss me. But now, underneath the cringe I was feeling, I felt calm. Maybe it was because when the threat of death by deranged fairy-tale character is hanging over you, kissing your old crush doesn't seem like a big deal. Maybe it was because John seemed so nervous and eager to do the right thing that he just made my anxiety disappear.

"I am," he said, his eyes looking straight into mine.

He sounded so serious that Romy laughed and said, "You're not getting married, you know!"

John glanced at Romy but didn't laugh. He swallowed hard and looked back at me. He looked . . . scared. Was it possible that he was scared of me? Did he know that it was my fault that he had turned into a beast? If he did, then of course he'd be scared of me. He *should* be scared of me.

"I'm really sorry, John," I said, remembering how

terrible he had looked in that hospital room. "I'm sorry about all of this."

"It's okay," he whispered.

And then, before I could think about what I was doing, I closed my eyes and leaned in to kiss him on the cheek.

Before I'd even made contact with John's face, Romy chimed in. "I think it needs to be on the lips. You know, like in the fairy tales."

I sighed. This wasn't how I'd pictured my first kiss. But having Romy beside us—she was inches from my and John's faces—commenting and critiquing sort of made things easier. Like there was no way this could be romantic. Maybe it wouldn't even count as my first kiss.

Like ripping off a bandage, I kissed John on the lips. And I didn't feel anything. Not a flicker of the thrill I'd felt when he'd showed up with my scrunchie. Not a burst of magic or energy to show that the kiss had done something to the spell.

"Now John kisses you," said Romy matter-of-factly.

I shot an annoyed look at Romy.

"Just in case that's what needs to happen," said Romy firmly. "Juuust to be sure."

"You okay with this?" asked John nervously. "Me kissing you?"

I nodded, wishing he looked a bit more excited about it, instead of looking like he was about to get a dental exam.

He kissed me on the lips. And I didn't feel anything.

So, that was that.

John sat back down on the step and sighed. He seemed as relieved as I was that it was over. A couple of days ago, kissing John was a dream that I hadn't even dared to think about. Now, I'd done it. I'd kissed him. But all I felt was disappointment. I missed the Cia of a few days ago, who got giddy whenever she thought about John. It seemed like that girl was gone forever.

"Do you feel anything?" asked Romy.

"No," I said. But I didn't know what I was supposed to feel. This was the first time I'd ever tried to break a spell.

"Okay," said Romy. "Let's check on your hair."

I shook my head and ran my hand through my hair, gasping as masses of it fell onto the stone floor. Romy's shriek and the appalled look on her face confirmed what I already knew. I hadn't broken the spell. If anything, I had accelerated it. I lifted my hands up and grabbed the top of my head. There was no hair. Only skin. I moved my hands around the sides of my head and the nape of my neck. Same story. I was completely bald. I let out a little whimper of despair.

"It doesn't really look that bad," said John softly. I turned my head away from both of them, wiping at a tear that spilled over onto my cheek. Why was I crying? It was just hair.

"I'm sorry it didn't work," said Romy, taking off the baseball cap she was wearing and placing it carefully on my head.

It wasn't Romy's fault. And anyway, my baldness was now the least of our worries. Somewhere above us, either on the other side of the trapdoor or the small barred windows—I couldn't tell exactly—there was a chorus of whistling.

They were back.

Chapter 19

LOOKED AROUND THE BASEMENT AGAIN, SEEING if I had missed something that could save us or at *least* help us. This couldn't be happening. There had to be a way out. Was there something heavy I could throw at them? Or something we could use to barricade the door? We were three kids about to go up against seven bone-crushingly strong giants. We didn't stand a chance. It didn't even feel dramatic to think that I wasn't ready to die. It would break my parents' hearts, and Riley would hate being an only child. I was his big sister, and he needed me. I'd just started reading him the first Percy Jackson. I had to stick around to finish the whole series.

Romy and John were running around the basement holding up their phones, desperately trying to find a signal.

"I'll try your phone again, Cia," he said, holding out a hand to me.

I looked at John and noticed the kind, worried expression on his face. It was totally different from the boy I had seen in the hospital bed the day before. That wasn't the real John. The real John was the kind, smart guy I'd thought he was. And he'd probably—it was possible—liked me all along.

Suddenly I knew what I had to do. It was our only chance of getting out of this mess.

I closed my eyes and silently apologized to John for what was about to happen. I hoped he would understand that I had had no choice. I realized that he might hate me forever, that we'd never exchange a real kiss, that he might never speak to me again. But there was nothing else I could do.

I closed my eyes and forced myself to think about how

brown John's eyes looked when he wore a navy sweater, how cute he'd looked a few minutes ago when he told me he was sorry, the way my heart used to skip a beat whenever I spotted him at school. I dug deep inside to find the crush I had buried.

I opened my eyes to see if it was working.

It was. John was hunched over as if he had just been punched in the stomach. Hair was sprouting on his arms and face, his shoulders were getting wider, and he was growing taller. Horns appeared at the top of his head. He threw his head back and let out a roar.

The beast was back. And this time it didn't seem like there was any John left.

"Cia!" shouted Romy. "What did you do?"

"He's our only way out," I explained, dashing over to John. "Remember what he said about wanting to smash things when he was 'sick'?

"Are you strong enough to bust that door open?" I asked beastly John, pointing up the steps.

Without answering, John cleared the stairs in two strides and slammed into the door, breaking it in half. He continued through the opening, and Romy and I ran after him back into the room where I had had my meeting with Snow White.

"There's another door up ahead!" I screamed at John, hoping he'd blast through the front door with the same efficiency as the trapdoor. The three of us rushed on, heading for the front of the cottage. It was in our sights when it opened, and Shiny and her awful crew stepped over the threshold.

John stopped suddenly, leaned forward, and pawed the stone floor like a bull getting ready to charge. He rushed, sending Shiny and the other cleaners scattering like pins hit by a bowling ball.

"Just get her! The bald one!" screamed Snow White, who had run into the hallway.

Romy and I charged through the gap that John had made, jumping over the cleaners who were sprawled out on the ground. I had almost made it to the spot where Romy and John had left their bikes when an arm reached across my neck from behind. I was lifted up in the air, and, gasping for breath, I tried to kick my attacker with the backs of my legs as I was dragged toward Snow White's cottage. John leapt on top of us and pinned my attacker—I think it was Speckless—to the ground as I rolled out of the way and headed toward the bikes.

Panting, Romy was leaning over her bike. She lifted an arm, and I looked back to see what she was pointing at.

The cleaners were attacking John, and he was dispatching each of them one by one with a punch or a well-aimed headbutt or a body slam. Snow White, who was standing on the doorstep of the cottage, fuming, had to jump out of the way of the two gigantic dwarfs he threw over his shoulder.

"Let's get out of here," said Romy, running toward the white van.

"John, let's go!" I yelled.

He ran toward me and grabbed his bike. It looked like a toddler trike in his huge paws.

"Forget about the bike," roared Romy. "I've got a better idea!" She was leaning out of the driver's seat of the white van. "Get in." She revved the engine.

For a fraction of a second I marveled at the fact that Romy was ready to drive what was about to be our getaway vehicle. (We were both about three years away from getting our driver's permits.) But this wasn't the time for questions. I pulled back the side door of the van and scrambled inside, with John jumping in behind me. As I leaned over to pull the door shut, Snow White strode toward the van, her navy dress billowing out behind her, eyes flashing angrily.

"I'll get you for this! This is not playing fair!"

Did she mean hijacking her van, or using a massive beast to escape? Under the circumstances I thought both methods were extremely fair.

I waved her goodbye and slammed the door shut.

"When did you start driving?" I asked Romy as the van lurched forward, whacking my chin into the back of the driver's seat. I reached back and got my seat belt on just before we came screeching to a sudden stop.

"Sorry!" shouted Romy. "Pulled the hand brake there instead of the gear stick." There was a roar of the engine revving, and then we were off again, careening down a quiet residential street.

"Romy, do you know what you're doing?" I asked, forcing my voice to sound calm. Romy was clearly way too small for the driver's seat. Which made sense, since the last person in that seat had been seven feet tall. She was steering with her fingertips because the steering wheel was so far away, and the seat was so low to the ground that her eyes were just about level with the dashboard.

"I got it," she said, sticking her tongue out the way she always did when she was doing something she found immensely difficult. It was not a reassuring look.

"But when did you start driving?" I asked again.

"Last summer," she answered, looking at me in the rearview mirror. (I kind of wished she'd keep her eyes on the road.) "There's a jeep at the cottage, and Noah's been teaching me to drive."

The "cottage" was Romy's family's sprawling estate in upstate New York. It had an ice rink, a baseball field, and an apple orchard.

"And I haven't crashed in ages," she said, coming within millimeters of taking off the side mirror of a parked car.

"That was awesome," said John, punching the back of the seat in front of him. His hand/claws went right through it, pulling out the upholstered insides. "Who are we going to fight next? Bring it on!"

"Cia, you need to do something about him," said Romy.

"Okay. I know," I muttered. Now that we had put some distance between us and Snow White's sidekicks, I needed to turn him back into a seventh-grade boy.

I glanced over at beastly John. Stuffed into the back seat beside me, his knees were hitting his chin, his elbows crammed against the window on one side and on top of Romy's bike—which was wedged between us—on the other. The sweatshirt and jeans he'd been wearing were ripped and now way too small for him. He reminded me of the Hulk after the transformation from mild-mannered scientist to huge green monster, except John was huge *and* hairy. He looked really, really uncomfortable. I felt so bad for what I'd done to him.

But sympathy was not the way to go. I wouldn't be able to change him back with compassion. Once again closing my eyes, I channeled how angry I had felt in the hospital room. How much I had hated him. I needed to feel that way again. I forced myself to replay what he had said, thinking about the cruel look in his eyes and the horrible laughter, but as soon as I got a handle on those memories, thoughts of the sincere apology he gave me and the kindness I saw in his face started to nibble at the edges of my brain. I tried to push those images away, but the good stuff kept coming. Now that I knew he hadn't meant what he had said in the hospital room, how could I keep on hating him? Now that I knew he had gone to my house to say sorry, how could I not like him?

This was, I realized with a sickening feeling, what our English teacher called a catch-22. I finally understood what Mr. Acevedo had been trying to explain to us for the last couple of weeks. *A catch-22 is a situation when a desired outcome is impossible to achieve because of a set of illogical rules.* My desired outcome was to turn John back into a boy, and the rules were that in order to achieve that outcome, I had to dislike him, but I couldn't make myself dislike him. The only way to change him back into a boy was to *not* want him to change back into a boy.

I felt like banging my head against the back of Romy's seat.

I don't like John Lee. John Lee is awful. I don't like John Lee. I don't have a crush on John Lee.

I repeated this over and over again in my head. But it was no good. The words made no difference to my heart.

"Romy," I said, "I'm trying. But I can't do it. I can't change him back."

"Okay, okay," said Romy, sticking her tongue out again. "I'll take him to my house. We need to hide him."

Romy was right—no one could see him like this. Not his father, not a doctor. No one. How would we explain that he was now the beast from the "Beauty and the Beast" story? No one would ever believe us.

"Cia," said Romy, her voice cracking in a way I'd never heard before. "If you can't change him back, you need to break the spell."

I needed to break the spell. It was the first time Romy had said those words. In all the time she'd spent strategizing and supporting me since that first meeting with Madame Fredepia, Romy had never said, "*You* need to break the spell." She had never made it my responsibility. But she was right. It was my responsibility. I had deliberately turned John into a snorting, angry, hairy beast. I had to find a way to change him back. I thought about everything I had just learned—that Snow White and the other fairy-tale princesses were real, that Madame Fredepia was a fairy godmother and she wasn't the only one. There was a whole league of them. Where were they?

What else had Snow White said? Princesses don't break spells. We're not the ones with the magic. *We're not the ones with the magic.*

It was true, wasn't it? The Evil Queen, not Snow White, was the one who cast spells. The villains were always the ones with magic. The ones you'd want to see if you needed something magicky done. And now that I knew the princesses were real, living right here in our world, among us . . . surely the villains were too, right?

All I needed to do was track one down.

Chapter 20

R OMY," I SAID, "I NEED TO GO HOME."

I quickly outlined what I'd been thinking about fairy-tale villains. I needed to get back up to the attic to go through Mom's papers. Maybe there'd be something in the pile of paperwork about the Evil Queen, or Cinderella's stepmother, or the Sea Witch, or the sorcerer from "Aladdin." I pulled out my phone. I'd try Mom again to see if she knew anything about how I might be able to find a (helpful) villain.

"I'm on it!" shouted Romy, slamming on the brakes. "It's less than a mile away. Get you there in two minutes."

She swung the van so sharply to the left that I jolted forward, almost falling onto the gear stick.

"Oh no, I think we've got a tail," said Romy. She was glancing back and forth between the road and the rearview mirror.

"What?" I gasped, putting my phone back into my pocket. I couldn't call Mom now. What was Romy talking about? Was the van sprouting feathers? What fairy tale was that from? "What do you mean?"

"A tail!" she repeated. "Haven't you ever seen a spy movie? We're being followed! There's a car behind us that just turned too."

I looked over my shoulder and out the window. There was a pink car within inches of the back of the van. It was so close, I could see the driver clearly. Blond hair, big lashes, slightly manic smile. She waved a hand at me and mouthed something that I couldn't make out. I recognized her—it was the high schooler from the parking lot.

"Let's shake her," said Romy, making a hairpin turn that threw me on top of John. He glared at me, and I scooted back over to my side of the seat.

I felt a thump and heard glass breaking as the van came to a sudden stop.

"We've been hit!" squealed Romy.

John leaned forward and roared. It was a deep, terrifying sound, like something a lion would make to show all the other lions who was boss. And if this had been Africa, the roar would have been no big deal. But we were in Brooklyn, and there were hundreds of people within shouting distance who would have heard that roar. We needed to get John out of here. Fast.

I glanced out the back window again. The girl was rubbing her head. She looked like she might have been hurt.

"You get John out of here!" I shouted at Romy. "I'll make sure the driver's okay. I know her. Sort of. And I can walk home from here."

"I got it," said Romy. "I'll take care of John. You figure out how to break the spell."

I slid the van door open and jumped out.

Romy revved the van. I smelled burning rubber, and then, leaving a cloud of exhaust fumes behind them, they were gone.

I walked over to the pink car and knocked on the window. The girl looked over at me and rolled down her window.

"Are you okay?" I said.

"I just chipped a nail," she said, lifting up a hand and wriggling her fingers. She smiled at me. "But you"—she leaned out of the car—"are you okay?"

She said it so sincerely and looked at me so warmly that I thought I might start crying.

"Well . . . ," I began, not sure what to say. "I really need to get home now . . . if you're okay." I needed to track down a villain ASAP.

She opened the car door and stepped out. Then she gave me a hug.

"That Snow White—she's a piece of work, isn't she?" she said.

She knew Snow White? Who was this girl?

"How do you know about Snow White?" I asked. "I mean, you know"—I wanted to make sure she and I were talking about the same thing—"that she's here in Brooklyn?"

"Well, yeah," said the girl, reaching into a tiny purse she had slung over her shoulder and taking out a pack of gum. She offered me a piece. I shook my head. I didn't think I could chew gum and think at the same time. "I wouldn't usually have time to worry about Snow White because of"—she paused and looked at me conspiratorially—"well, you know who, but now that you've taken *her* out of the running, I have time to check on the rest of the competition."

What was she talking about?

"I was just parked outside Snow White's place. I was going to follow the cleaning crew when they left to see whose house they were going to. They have some really quality customers, you know?" She paused, smacking on her gum.

No, I didn't know.

"Like, millionaires and stuff, not actual princes . . . but still . . . good enough."

Now I understood what she was talking about. I felt like I was back with Snow White listening to her lecture on how to get a rich husband. But why was this girl talking about this? Wasn't she still in high school? Why was she staking out Snow White's house trying to track down an eligible husband?

She nodded at her car and said, "So, I was just sitting in TruLuv here when the front door burst open and you came running out with your friend and that big hairy guy, and all those dwarfs were trying to stop you. And Snow White—" The girl started laughing so much, she couldn't speak. "And Snow White was so mad. She was stomping her feet and stuff, and it was awesome!"

The girl grinned at me.

"And you did it! You made another princess so mad. You're like a princess-busting superhero."

This was weird. Who was this girl? Why was a high schooler so interested in fairy-tale princesses? Before I could ask, she kept on going.

"So, I called my sister—she just loves you too—and I told her what had just happened with Snow White, and she said I had to go thank you. For both of us. So, I took off to try to catch you, and sorry I hit you, but, well, here you are now. So, thank you!"

She hugged me again.

"You have a sister?" I asked. I could feel my heart thumping a little faster. I think I knew who I was talking to. "The girl you were with in the parking lot?"

She nodded.

"But you have another sister? A stepsister?"

She nodded sulkily this time.

"And that sister," I continued, wanting to be absolutely sure, "is Cinderella?"

"Cinder-annoying, Cinder-oh-so-perfect-ella, Cinder-pain-in-the-butt . . . ," said the girl. "That's her."

"Can you tell me your name again?" I said. I couldn't believe it. I needed to get to a fairy-tale villain, and now, standing in front of me, was one of the daughters of one of the big ones.

Cinderella's stepmother.

"It's Hildee," she said. "And you're Cia, right?"

I nodded.

"Hildee, do you think I could meet your mother? I'd really like to talk to her about, you know . . ."

I was about to say *fairy-tale stuff*, but before I could finish, Hildee started talking.

"Of course. We've told her all about you. She'd, like, love to meet you, and I've gotta get home for afternoon tea anyway. She's a big fan of your work, you know?"

I wasn't sure having the evil stepmother as a "fan" was

a good thing, but either way I had to meet her. She was a villain. She'd know how to break a spell, wouldn't she?

"C'mon," said Hildee, opening her car door. "My house is just a few blocks from here."

I walked over to the other side of the car, opened the door, and sat down in the passenger's seat.

"Let's go," I said. I had a villain to meet.

Chapter 21

A S WE DROVE, I THOUGHT ABOUT HOW TO BEST bring up the topic of spell-breaking with Hildee's mother. But it was hard to think when Hildee had turned on the radio at top volume and was singing along to the music.

"You gotta shake, shake, shake it," she belted out, swaying from side to side.

"Shake, shake, shake it!" The tune and the words burst out of me soprano-style before I knew what was happening.

"Whoa!" said Hildee. "That was beautiful! You have an amazing voice."

I reached over and turned off the radio.

"Please, can we just not have any music?" I said. "It doesn't really agree with me."

"Okay," said Hildee, throwing me a questioning look.

"Thanks." I'd thought that staying away from water and not singing would stop my tail from kicking in. But what if just *hearing* music would make me sing, and then that would activate the tail? I'd just heard that bit of music on the radio, and the song erupted out of me. Almost as if I'd hiccuped. I couldn't stop it.

"'S okay," said Hildee. "I feel that way about dancing. But you do have an amazing voice."

"Thank you," I said, staring out the window. We were in a fancy neighborhood a bit like the one where Romy lived. All the houses had miniature trees in fancy pots, standing like soldiers at the entrances. The doorknobs gleamed, the black railings in front of each house shone as if they had just been freshly painted, and even the cats—whom I spotted on the steps of a few houses—looked very well-fed and groomed.

"This is it," said Hildee, pulling up in front of a beautiful three-story brownstone.

She parked the car, and we both got out. I followed

her up a flight of steps to the front door that had a bronze plaque on it that said CHARMING CONNECTIONS—the two Cs overlapped like wedding rings—and underneath, there were the words FIND YOUR HAPPILY EVER AFTER.

"Charming Connections?" I asked Hildee.

"Oh, that's Mom's business," she said.

Cinderella's stepmother was a professional matchmaker? That was a bit of a surprise. Why did her daughters make such a fuss about finding husbands if their mother was in the romance business?

I looked at my reflection in the bronze plaque. It wasn't good. The cap Romy had given me looked like I'd sat on it, I had splinters of wood—probably bits of the trapdoor that John had blasted through—scattered like dandruff on my shoulders, and there were smears of dirt across my cheeks. No wonder Hildee had looked so concerned when she'd asked me if I was okay. I looked terrible. I adjusted my cap, dusted off my shoulders, and wiped my face with the bottom of my sweatshirt. It didn't change much, but it was the best I could do.

Hildee opened the front door, and I walked in after her into a beautiful hallway. It looked like one of those rooms in a magazine or a movie, the ones my mom had always assured me didn't actually exist because, according to her, no one really lived like that, surrounded by vases of fresh flowers and perfectly plumped cushions and gleaming surfaces. Well, Mom was wrong. This place was all those things and more.

"Welcome."

The owner of the posh voice appeared from the other end of the hallway. She was a tall, elegant woman dressed in a cream Chanel suit with a choker of pearls around her neck. She had shoulder-length gray hair that didn't match her face, which seemed to have no wrinkles.

"I'm Lady Graff," she said.

This was another first. I'd never met a "lady" before. I felt like I was making progress, finally. This was better than meeting another princess; Lady Graff would know what to do.

"I'm Cia," I said, shaking the hand that she extended toward me. I took in the dazzling display of pearls and diamonds on her wrist. Suddenly I felt intensely aware of my appearance and the fact that I was horribly under-dressed. I pulled at the bottom of my sweatshirt in a pointless attempt to smooth out the wrinkles.

"You look like you've had a terrible time," she said, her hand hovering over my shoulder, like she wanted to give me a comforting tap but couldn't quite bring herself to touch me. "Let's have some tea."

She led me into a room that was even lovelier than the hallway—more fresh flowers in vases, plumped cushions, and gleaming surfaces. She pointed at a paisley-patterned armchair, and I sat down. Despite the fact that I knew I was in the presence of a certified villain, it felt nice to take a break. I was looking forward to a cup of tea. And maybe there'd be cookies, too? I smiled at Lady Graff. Snow White, who was supposed to be sweet and kind, had been a nightmare, so maybe Lady Graff, who was supposed to be conniving and cruel, would be the opposite. A warm, welcoming, and helpful hostess?

When she rang a tiny silver bell, I expected a maid to show up, but instead Hildee reappeared, sticking her head around the doorway.

"We'll have a pot of tea," said her mother.

"Can't Wilhemina do it?" Hildee sighed, her shoulders slumping. "I did it last time."

"And it was too weak," said her mother. "You need more practice. Do it again." Lady Graff waved her hand dismissively, and Hildee disappeared around the doorway with another loud sigh.

"Well," said her mother, smiling at me. But it was one of those smiles that was all mouth. It didn't reach her eyes. "My girls have filled me in. You *have* upset Cinderella, haven't you? It's been such a treat seeing her so . . . discombobulated."

I nodded.

I didn't like the way she said "discombobulated" with a note of nasty glee in her voice. I might have to revise my theory that Lady Graff would not behave the way she did in the fairy tale. What did I know about Cinderella's stepmother? According to everything I'd read, she was awful. She might have even murdered Cinderella's father and the husband before him. And she'd been ruthless in her pursuit of the only available prince in the land for her daughters, even telling them to cut off bits of their feet so that they could fit into the glass slipper. All the Disney versions left out that part of the story, though.

Lady Graff clearly still hated Cinderella, and as I

had—albeit unintentionally—turned Cinderella's life upside down and made Cinderella hate me, didn't that make it likely that Lady Graff would want to help me? *My enemy's enemy is my friend* was what our history teacher had said when she was talking about how France helped George Washington fight the British. Hopefully that applied here, too.

I glanced around the room looking for a clock. (After the way she'd criticized Hildee's tea-making, I didn't dare pull out my phone in front of Lady Graff.) I wondered how long it had been since Romy had taken off with John in the van. Would they have made it back to her house by now? I hoped they were both okay.

"I was wondering if you might be able to help me with something," I said to Lady Graff. I needed to figure out how to break the spell fast. If John let out another roar, Romy's neighbors would definitely call the cops. How much time did I have before that happened?

"Continue," said Lady Graff, looking at me in an interested, but not especially encouraging, way.

I opened my mouth to speak, but there was a clatter of noise as Hildee walked into the room carrying an overloaded silver tray. The teacups clanged against the saucers and sugar bowl as she placed the tray on the table.

"There you go," she said, flopping down in an armchair, obviously exhausted from the effort of boiling water and carrying cups.

"Posture," snapped Lady Graff, whacking her daughter on the back with what looked like a riding crop. I winced. That looked like it hurt.

"Ouch!" yelled Hildee, rubbing her lower back and sitting up.

"Pour the tea," hissed her mother.

Hildee reached for the teapot. I tried to catch her eye to give her a grateful and sympathetic look, but she was too focused on pouring tea to see what I was doing.

I muttered a "thanks" and took my cup. It was overfilled, and tea slopped onto the saucer when I lifted the cup to my lips.

"Useless," said Lady Graff in a cold voice, glaring at Hildee. "Absolutely useless."

"Well, the thing is . . . ," I said, trying to balance my teacup and saucer on my knee. I wanted to get Lady Graff's attention off poor Hildee. "I was hoping that you might be able to help me break a spell. I don't know if you know, but I was spelled—that's what's causing all this magic meltdown—and I really need to break the spell. . . . Hildee, this tea is delicious, by the way." I smiled at her, and she looked down at her lap, but she had a tiny grin on her face.

"Well, don't look at me," said Lady Graff, arching one eyebrow. "I certainly can't help you." She was balancing her saucer and teacup perfectly.

"But can't you do magic?" I insisted. "You're a vill—I mean, you're . . . very powerful, aren't you—"

"Look," interrupted Lady Graff, raising her hand up like a traffic cop. "This isn't my area of expertise, all right? My line is *sabotage*, not magic. Or haven't you read the story? And anyway, why would I want to help you? This spell that you're in the grips of has eliminated some of the competition for my daughters. Cinderella has to deal with lawsuits and jail instead of hunting for a husband, so that means more eligible prospects for my daughters." She threw a withering look at Hildee, who seemed to have checked out of the conversation and was leafing through a magazine. "My daughters," she continued, speaking out of the side of her mouth in a stage whisper, "need all the help they can get."

So much for the *enemy of my enemy is my friend* theory.

I didn't know whether to sob or to scream. She really couldn't help me? I placed my cup and saucer on the table. The knee thing wasn't working. My hands had started trembling.

"It's all right for my fellow so-called villains," Lady Graff continued. "They don't have daughters to worry about." She threw another disgusted look at Hildee, whom I kept feeling worse for. Her mother was a nightmare. "They're building businesses and brands. . . . I have to focus on getting my girls married"—she took out the riding crop again and whacked it on the table as she spoke—"to"—*thwhack*—"the"—*thwhack*—"best"—*thwhack*—"possible"—*thwhack*—"man."

"Okay, okay," I said, getting up from my seat. I needed to get away from Lady Graff and her riding crop/weapon.

"Just look at Snow White's stepmother," said Lady Graff, getting to her feet and walking toward me. "Owns Forever Young. She isn't dealing with two slouches for daughters."

My heart skipped a beat.

"*She* owns Forever Young?" I said, trying to keep my voice casual. "The cosmetics company?"

"Obviously," said Lady Graff, waving a hand above her head theatrically. "And Gothel can focus on her security firm." She lifted up her hands to make quotation marks and then sang an annoying ad I must have heard on the car radio a thousand times. "'No one gets in or out with us. . . . That's the Gothel guarantee.'"

As if my voice had completely separated from my brain, I started humming along with her. I slapped my hand over my mouth to stop the singing.

She threw me a quizzical look and then continued.

"Even that bony battle-ax, the Sea Witch," she blurted out. "She's made a name for herself. Calls herself Selma Waterbury now. Has that swimming academy. Always in the magazines. Wheeling and dealing." She was getting more animated and annoyed as she spoke, waving her riding crop around. I glanced at Hildee, who was still absorbed by the magazine. She'd obviously heard all this before.

I'd heard of the Selma Waterbury Academy, hadn't I? I was almost sure it was in New York. My mind began racing. How I could get away from Lady Graff and find a villain with real magic?

Lady Graff threw the riding crop on the table.

"They don't have daughters. They don't have to worry the way I have to worry. I can't be a titan of industry." She paused dramatically and clutched her pearls. "I have to get my girls married."

"Well," I said, moving toward the door, "best of luck with that. This has been very interesting. Thanks very much for the tea."

Within a fraction of a second, Lady Graff had gotten to her feet, beating me to the door.

"Sit down and finish your tea," she snapped. "And you," she shouted at Hildee. "Keep her here until I get back. I have a wake to attend. The widower is very rich. I have to move fast because those New York women will be circling him like vultures."

She grabbed a fur-trimmed cream cape from the back of a chair, threw it over her shoulders, and then walked out the door, the cape flying out behind her like wings. The door slammed behind her, and I heard the click of a key turning as she locked it on the other side.

Feeling desperate, I tried to turn the handle, but it didn't budge. I banged on the door and yelled, "Hey! You can't do this! Let me out!"

"I wouldn't bother," said Hildee, not looking up from her magazine. "She's not going to let you out."

"But I have to go!" I said, still pulling at the handle. "I have to get out of here."

I ran over to the huge windows that overlooked the street. I pushed one open and looked out at the ten-foot drop to the ground below. Jumping wasn't an option.

I considered calling the police, but I didn't know how much time I had left before John let out a roar or—even worse—managed to break out of Romy's house and get spotted. I didn't want to be chatting with law enforcement while he was making international headlines.

"Hildee," I said, trying to keep the panic out of my voice. "Can you please let me out of here?"

"Sorry, can't," she said. She was now alternating between leafing through the magazine and scrolling through her phone. The magazine's cover said *America's Most Eligible Bachelors* underneath a collage of men engaged in eligible bachelor activities like waterskiing and polo and wine-drinking and standing on their enormous yachts. It was sort of familiar—I had probably seen it in line at the grocery store or something.

"But it's not for me," I pleaded. "If I can't get out of here, a boy in seventh grade is going to be a beast forever."

"Sucks for him," said Hildee, shrugging her shoulders. "If that's his story, that's his story."

That wasn't fair. It wasn't John's fault that he was turning into a beast.

"And I'll look like this forever," I said, whipping off my cap in what I hoped was a dramatic, effective play for sympathy. I really was past caring about the state of my hair—or lack thereof. Being bald did not seem like a big deal now that I thought about what John—and Romy—were dealing with, but it might mean something to Hildee, who, judging by her super-straight, bleach-blond hairstyle, spent a lot of time on it.

She gasped loudly at my reveal. "That's awful," she said, eyes wide with horror.

"Yeah," I said. I looked down at the ground, playing it up. "And if I can't get out to break the spell, I'll never have hair again."

"But if you do break the spell, wouldn't that mean that Cinderella will start being all Cinderella-y again?" She must have been listening to my conversation with Lady Graff after all. "And then Cinderella will . . . you know . . . get the prince. Again," she said, looking so heartbreakingly sad that it was impossible not to feel sorry for her. "I'm always the loser. I never get picked."

"But Hildee, there is no prince," I said. I couldn't believe I was having this conversation.

"Yes, there is," she said, waving the magazine at me.

"Well, then, there are loads of them," I said. I pointed at the front of the magazine where the number *300* was circled on the cover. "There's enough for all of you. If that's what you really want."

"It's not about want." She pouted. "It's the happily ever after. If we don't get a happily ever after, we—we're failures. And we have to have a prince to get our happily ever after."

"But—what if you don't *want* a prince? What if you don't like anyone? What if you don't want to get married?"

"Well, what else am I supposed to do?" said Hildee irritably.

"Hildee, you can do anything you want!" The words of that poster Mom put in my room popped into my head. "You can—you can write your own story."

"Write my own story," snorted Hildee. "That's ridiculous." She turned her attention back to the magazine and held out a page to show me a photo of a guy in a cowboy hat flashing big white teeth. "What do you think about him?" she mused.

"It says here his dream woman would love horses and hiking. Do you even like horses?" I wasn't going to ask about hiking. I was pretty sure that Hildee would hate any activity that jeopardized her nails.

"I could," she said with a determined edge to her voice. "Whatever. I could love horses." She kept flicking through the pages, moving on to the next eligible bachelor.

I stared at Hildee, suddenly feeling so sorry for her. She was almost out of high school, and she didn't even know whether or not she liked horses. For the rest of her life, she'd just like and do whatever she thought would get her a "prince." She had a mother who told her the point of her life was to marry rich, so Hildee didn't know what she wanted. Did she even know about all the other stuff she could do?

I'd been so mad at Mom for getting overexcited when I was interested in something and for giving me books about teenagers fighting climate change and starting businesses and just being amazing. All that had made me feel like she didn't think I was already amazing, but maybe she just wanted me to know that anything was possible, that I could do whatever I wanted. Maybe Mom didn't want me to win a Nobel prize. Maybe she just didn't want me to be like Hildee.

"Hildee," I said, determined to get her to see that there were lots of things she could do with her life. Endless possibilities! I almost felt as serious about getting Hildee to understand that she didn't have to get married as I did about breaking the spell. "You know you could go to college. Or you could be a performer!" She'd been so happy in the car singing along to the music. "Or you could do something in fashion. . . ." The two times I'd met her, she'd looked like she'd stepped out of the pages of a magazine. Maybe she should be *in* a magazine. "And you're just really nice, you know? You're so friendly. You could just do something where you get to chat to people."

Hildee lit up as I was talking, but then her face dropped. "Mother wouldn't like it."

"Your mother . . . ," I began, but was interrupted by my phone buzzing. I pulled it out of my back pocket. There was a text from Romy. And a photo. It was of holes in a door.

John did this. With his hands.

His HANDS!

I stared at the photo again. I recognized the door. It was in the home studio that Noah had set up. The door was super thick because the room was soundproof. John had just punched through it. Repeatedly. I counted twelve holes.

Another text from Romy.

He's getting worse.

Lady Graff had been a dead end, and I *needed* to get out of here and find out how to break the spell. I looked over at Hildee. She was still frowning, no doubt thinking about how much "Mother" would hate her doing anything that didn't increase her chances of getting a prince. How long would it take me to persuade Hildee that she didn't have to listen to her mother? But I didn't have time for that. I had to get out of here, fast. If John was busting through soundproof doors, it wouldn't be long before Romy's neighbors called the police, and then . . .

"Hildee! I know how you can get to the best one," I said, pointing at the magazine. I silently begged Romy and Noah and the rest of their family for forgiveness for what I was about to do. And Hildee, too. I was pushing her right back onto the track I wished she'd get off. "Top twenty anyway."

A look of confusion flickered across Hildee's face, followed quickly by excitement.

"What?" she said, holding the magazine to her chest. "In here?"

"Noah Agarwal," I said. "He's number fourteen."

I'd finally figured out why I'd recognized the magazine. Romy had told me about how upset all her family—especially Noah—had been when Noah got included on the list. They were furious about having his name and photo plastered on its pages.

Hildee lifted a finger, licked it, and then flipped through the pages as if her life depended on it.

"Him?" she shouted, holding up a page that had a grainy, out-of-focus shot of Noah coming out of a Starbucks. "He's gorgeous! You know him?"

"His sister is my best friend," I said. "Let me out of here, and I'll . . . I'll find a way for you to meet him."

"Just me," she said. "Not my sister?"

"Of course," I said. "Just you."

"And you won't tell Cinderella?" asked Hildee warily.

"I don't even . . ." I was about to say *know Cinderella*, but I stopped myself. "No, I won't say anything. She's not his type anyway."

I didn't know who Noah's type was, but my comment seemed to make Hildee delighted.

"Deal!" she said. She walked over to the windows, reached behind the linen drapes, and took out a key.

As I ran out the hallway and down the front steps, I heard her shout behind me, "Hope you get your hair back!"

Chapter 22

I PULLED OUT MY PHONE AND FIGURED OUT THE location of the nearest subway station. I had to get to another villain. One who had real magic and wasn't so obsessed with getting her daughters a "royal" match. As I ran, my phone started to ring. It was Dad.

"Cia, what is going on?" he shouted. "Your mom called when she landed in LA. Says you hung up on her. She's worried sick."

"I'm fine, Dad," I said. I was within a few feet of the subway station. "I have to go to history now." I hung up.

261

It was shocking how easy it was for me to lie. I called Mom's number. Voicemail again.

I got to the station and cleared the steps three at a time. When I got to the ticket machines, I pulled out my phone and typed in *Selma Waterbury Academy*. I was right—I *had* passed it before. The address for the Selma Waterbury Academy was only six stops away. Lady Graff had said the Sea Witch was always "wheeling and dealing." She was in the business of bartering; I knew that much from the fairy tale. So maybe I could offer her a deal. She'd break the spell, and I'd . . . Well, I didn't know what my side of the deal could be. I'd figure that out later.

When I sat down in the subway car, I sighed so loudly that the man sitting next to me glanced in my direction and then moved closer to the edge of his seat, putting as much space as possible between us. I checked out my reflection in the window and sighed again. I wouldn't have wanted to sit beside me either. I had a fierce *don't-mess-with-me* scowl on my face, and I looked like I'd been through a war zone, which I guess I had been. The bruises from my run-in with the giant dwarfs were starting to show.

I read through the text messages Mom had sent in the last couple of hours.

Stay away from Madame Fredepia!

It was a bit late for that.

Call me!

Cia, go home and wait for me there.

But how could I just go home and wait for Mom to get back when I knew I had a shot at breaking the spell now? Mom didn't know that there was a seventh-grade beast hidden in Romy's house. No, I wasn't going home. Not when I had a chance to meet a villain who might cure the boy I had cursed.

I texted Romy. **How's John?**

I did this, she replied.

I looked at a photo of John asleep on a sofa. His massive legs and arms were hanging over the sides.

I poured NyQuil into a bottle of Gatorade and gave it to him.

Romy! You can't drug people.

Well, you turned him into a beast.

Fair point. I had no comeback for that.

I stared at the photo of the beast that used to be John. At least he looked peaceful when he was sleeping. But he couldn't spend the rest of his life drugged up and hiding in people's garages.

How are you? texted Romy.

Met villain #1. Did not go well. On my way to #2 now.

She texted me a fingers-crossed emoji.

As my train pulled into the station, I sent one last text.

Is Noah dating anyone?

Then I read up on the Selma Waterbury Academy. Lady Graff's description of the Sea Witch as a swimming teacher was a gross understatement. It was like saying Van Gogh liked to make doodles of the night sky. She was the recipient of five lifetime achievement awards from the American Swimming Association. Her school had produced more Olympians than any other school in the country, and she had trained more gold medalists and world-record holders than any other swim coach in the *world*. According to the articles I skimmed, her teaching methods were shrouded in secrecy—anyone who wanted to train with her had to sign a nondisclosure agreement, which sounded super intense—and her techniques were controversial. One former swimmer who was quoted anonymously said that she ran a swimming sweatshop and called her a double-crossing witch. In recent years the Sea Witch's business interests had expanded beyond the swimming school. She was the mastermind and owner of the hottest and highest-grossing show in Las Vegas history, *Circus of the Sea*. I'd never heard of it. But then again, I don't exactly know what's hot in Las Vegas. I clicked on a show highlights video and watched a beautiful lady wearing a glittery swimsuit dive off a board into a deep pool that was about the same size as a bathtub. The drop was at least fifty feet from diving board to water, and on the way the lady sliced through three rings of fire while spinning herself around like a corkscrew. It was so amazing that I had to fight the temptation to tap my reluctant seatmate on the shoulder and show it to him.

The train was pulling in to my station as I was finishing up an article about Selma Waterbury making it onto the Forbes 400 Richest People in America list last year. I put my phone back into my pocket and stood up. I still didn't know how I was going to get what I wanted from the Sea Witch, but I hoped that inspiration would strike at the right moment, the way it had at the hospital with the red carnation and the elevator.

The swimming academy was just a few blocks from the station, and even if I hadn't had the address, I would have found it with my nose; the smell of chlorine was that strong. As I approached the entrance, the automatic glass doors slid open, and I stepped into a marble lobby that looked more like the foyer of a fancy hotel than a swimming school. Aware of how conspicuous I was—I did not look like an Olympic athlete, that was for sure—I walked up to the reception desk and read the sign that hung from the ceiling just above it.

LOSING IS FOR LOSERS.

The letters scrambled and changed. Now the sign said:

NO ONE LIKES LOSERS.

I coughed to get the attention of the man who was sitting behind the desk. He was wearing so much gel that his black hair looked wet. He had an earpiece in and was talking into the tiny microphone extension.

"Good afternoon. The Selma Waterbury Academy, fifty-six gold medals and counting . . . Hold, please."

I coughed again.

He raised an eyebrow and looked at me.

"I'm here to see the Sea . . . I mean, Selma Waterbury, please," I said.

"Appointment?"

"Yes," I lied.

"Really?" He raised the second eyebrow. "Name?"

"Cia Anderson."

"You don't have an appointment, Ms. Anderson," he said without even glancing at his computer or the book on his desk. "No meetings with Mrs. Waterbury without an appointment."

He pointed at the double doors I'd just entered through, indicating that he was finished with our conversation.

"Actually, could I just use the restroom, please?" I asked innocently. "Before I leave." He wasn't getting rid of me that easily. The desperation and exhaustion was either making me braver than I usually was, or maybe I was just beyond the point of caring about what anyone thought of me. I didn't care that the receptionist thought—I could tell by the expression on his face—that I shouldn't even be breathing the same air as him. (I wondered if I smelled as bad as I looked. It was possible. I'd been sweating nonstop since the cleaning ladies/dwarfs had stuffed me in the carpet.)

"That way," he said, narrowing his eyes and looking at me suspiciously. He nodded to the left.

I walked in the direction he had pointed, moving slowly so that I could take in the layout. There was a sweeping staircase—it looked very out of place, like something that you'd see on a fancy cruise ship—and at the top of it was a big glass room that extended out over the lobby like a balcony. I saw a shadow of movement inside it. Whoever was in there would have an unobstructed view of everything that went on in the academy.

I got to the restroom, which was all gleaming white and shiny with regular sinks and stalls, but one thing was missing. There were no mirrors.

A tall girl came out of one of the stalls. She had on a white robe and a swim cap that said I'M A WINNER. She nodded at me.

"You here for the tryouts?" she said.

I stared at her blankly.

"Yeah, I was pretty freaked out too," said the girl. "But you get used to it. After a few days I didn't really mind anymore." She touched her cap. "And I kind of see the point of it now. It's a way of proving that you're really serious about entering the academy. Coach Waterbury wants to know you'll do anything to win."

"Okay," I said. I didn't know what she was talking about. But I *was* really serious about meeting Selma Waterbury, and I'd do anything—well maybe not *anything*, but I'd give a lot, like all my worldly possessions, or offer to clean the pool for a year, or name my first child after her. So, almost anything, if she would just break the counterspell.

"Get through that bit, then you have an interview with Coach Waterbury, and if she likes you, you get in the pool and race."

So getting in the pool was only required after the interview. That was a relief, at least. I just needed to ace the first part of the tryout—whatever that was—to get the meeting I needed.

"Good luck," said the girl. Then, noticing my confused look, she said, "You just go through there."

I followed her gaze to a door at the other end of the restroom.

"Thanks," I said, walking toward it, my anxiety rising as I wondered what could possibly be waiting for me on the other side.

Opening the door, I found that it was just a hallway. There was a line of ten girls standing by the wall, and I joined the end of it. They were giving off that nervous, jittery energy that I was used to from basketball tryouts when we had to line up to meet with the coach to find out what team we were on. The girl in front of me was twirling her long red hair and muttering, "I can do this. I can do this." A little ways up the line, a girl stepped out and said, "I've changed my mind!" and ran off down the hallway.

A large woman in a velour sweat suit with a whistle around her neck came walking down the hallway, pushing a chair on rollers that had a massive trash bag attached to it.

"Quiet!" she shouted, though no one had been speaking. She blew on her whistle. "Who's first?" She held up what looked like a TV remote.

"I'll do it," said the girl in front of me. She sat on the chair and closed her eyes. The sweat-suited woman turned on the TV remote, and I realized it wasn't a TV remote. It was an electric razor.

Within seconds, all the girl's beautiful red hair was on

the floor. She reached up and gingerly touched her head, wincing a little at the feel of the buzz cut she had just been given.

"Coach Waterbury will see you now. Take the stairs to the very top," said the sweat-suited woman, pointing at another door. The girl stood up and walked through it.

"I'm next!" I said before anyone else had a chance to volunteer. I ran to the chair and sat down, almost giddy with the realization that my entry ticket to get an interview with the Sea Witch was right under my hat.

I whipped off my baseball cap.

Some of the girls in the line gasped.

"Nice," said the woman. "Saved me the trouble. You can go see Coach Waterbury."

I walked through the same door the (formerly?) red-headed girl had just gone through. But when I was only halfway up the stairs, the girl came running down, tears streaming from her eyes.

"She said I don't have what it takes. She just took one look at me and sent me away! She said my toes were too long." She gulped. "I didn't even get a chance to speak."

I paused, taking in what the girl had just said. And as

I cleared the final steps of the stairs, I told myself to be careful, be very careful.

Heart hammering, I stepped over the threshold of the Sea Witch's lair.

All the walls of the office were made of glass. On one side there was a view of the foyer, and on the other a view of an Olympic-sized pool, separated into lanes filled with swimmers speeding through the water like dolphins chasing fish.

The Sea Witch was standing by her desk with her back to me. There was a fish tank, like an enormous marble bathtub, in the center of the office—I'd need to keep clear of that—and the Sea Witch walked over to it. She either hadn't noticed me standing by the door or she was ignoring me. Thin and carrying herself like a queen, she glided across the floor as if she were wearing roller skates. Maybe she was. I couldn't see her feet. She wore a shapeless but expensive-looking grayish blue dress that skimmed the floor, rings on every finger, and an elaborate green necklace that looked like calcified seaweed but was so shiny, it might have been made of emeralds. Her gray hair had shimmers of green throughout and was styled into a Cleopatra-style bob/helmet that looked stiff enough to hold up in a tsunami.

Her fingers skimmed the surface of the water in the tank, and a revolting eel-like creature poked its head out. She stroked its back like it was a dog and cooed at it. I got the sense that she knew I was in the room but was purposefully making me wait.

"Who's a lovely little sea serpent? Who loves his momsie?" The eel wrapped itself around the Sea Witch's wrist and forearm. She walked away from the tank toward the glass windows that overlooked the pool, wearing the serpent like it was a bracelet.

Then she turned around and looked at me.

"You're not here for a tryout," she said, giving me an appraising look. "You want something else."

Chapter 23

BEFORE I HAD A CHANCE TO COME UP WITH A response, the Sea Witch continued.

"You've come to see me about that," she said, gesturing at me and moving her hand up and down. I guessed she was able to see the yellow aura or whatever it was called that Madame Fredepia had said was shining off me. I decided to get right to the point.

"Yes," I said. I was proud that my voice wasn't shaking one bit. "And I'm hoping you can break the counterspell."

A look of annoyance crossed her face.

"Of course I can break a counterspell," she said. "Nothing to it."

She banged on the window and yelled into a microphone attached to her ear.

"Tell Phillip to do twenty push-ups after each lap. He looks like a loser."

The Sea Witch turned back around and smiled, flashing her big teeth at me. They had a slightly greenish tint to them.

"Such stupidity. Amazing what they will do for a shiny piece of metal. But I can tell you're different. You want something bigger, don't you?" she said, winking at me as if we were in on a joke together.

I didn't think wanting to break a counterspell was "bigger" than wanting to win a medal at the Olympics, but I thought I'd better play along. I nodded.

"Come sit," she said, ushering me over to a green sofa covered with a pattern of the initials *SW*. I sat.

"Enough small talk," said the Sea Witch. She sat down beside me like we were the best of friends. "Let's get down to business."

She looked pointedly at my legs.

"I'll give you thirty percent," she said, handing me a sheaf of papers that she seemed to have pulled out of thin air. "I'll manage all publicity, operational issues, and transport. You'll get star billing, of course, and an entire floor at the Bellagio. Best hotel in Vegas. They can turn one of the sunken suites into a pool for you."

30 percent? A floor at the Bellagio? Sunken suites? I didn't know what she was talking about.

"And the hair situation," she continued. "Bald's not a good look for a mermaid. You just let me know what color you'd like, and I'll take care of it. Cascading blond curls would work well, I think."

"I don't want to be blond," I said. "Look, you don't understand. . . ."

"Fine, fine, you pick the color." She walked back over to the window and yelled into her earpiece again.

"Tell Natalie in lane five that she looks like a manatee!" She threw her head back and laughed.

"We'll bill you as the eighth wonder of the world," she said, a faraway look in her eyes. "It'll be the biggest act in Las Vegas. I'll—I mean—we'll make a fortune. Have you thought about a stage name? Something alliterative that goes with mermaid . . . Miranda, Miravelle, Maryola, Maryann. Imagine it surrounded with flashing lights. You'll have creative input, obviously."

"But that's not why I'm here. That's not what I want," I said, my heart seizing up with fear. What did this woman want from me?

The Sea Witch laughed and pointed a finger at me.

"You are quite the negotiator, aren't you?" She paused, steepling her fingers in front of her face. "You drive a hard bargain. Forty percent. I'll give you forty percent."

She walked to her desk and slammed her hands as if everything was all wrapped up, even though I hadn't agreed to anything. Then she stood up and glided back to the sofa. She reached out her hand toward me.

"That tail is happening. You can stick with me and stay this-side up. Because I'm the only one with the power to keep you here. Once that tail happens, you'll belong to them."

"Them?" I asked, working hard to stop my voice from shaking. It was a lost cause.

"The merpeople. You'll become one of them when

you get that tail. You'll have to go down below. But I can keep you here. Let's shake on it," she said, still holding her hand toward me.

I stared. Her fingernails, which were green and mossy—like they were covered in algae—had been filed to sharp, dangerous-looking points. Even if the Sea Witch was right about me having to live in the ocean when the tail kicked in, I'd prefer to take my chances with the mer-people than with her.

I had to get out of there. I needed to run while I still had legs. She—and the disgusting fish on her wrist—were looking at me the way Riley looked at a tub of double fudge ice cream.

"You've got yourself a deal," I said, working hard to make sure my voice didn't give away the feeling of terror that was growing in the pit of my stomach. Coming here was a huge mistake. "This is all really exciting stuff—I mean, wow—I just need to, you know, get some air. It's a lot to take in." I walked toward the door of the office. As soon as I was clear of her, I'd race down the stairs, run outside, and put as much distance as possible between me and the Sea Witch.

"You're not going anywhere," she said. She spoke in a voice that was so cold and terrifying that I felt each word like a blow. She held out both hands in front of her, and I felt a draft of wind push me against the windows that overlooked the pool.

"Get in the water." She pointed at the supersized bathtub/fish tank in the center of the room.

No! If I got into the water, it would be game over. I just knew that was all it would take, and I'd be headlining the freakiest act in Las Vegas. Just looking at that water made my legs tingle.

But the Sea Witch was blocking the door. If I made a dash for it, she'd just push me into the tank. I had to do something to get her out of the room.

"I didn't bring a swimsuit," I said, pulling at my sweatshirt. "Do you have something to lend me?"

The Sea Witch narrowed her eyes and looked at me suspiciously.

With a shake of her arm, the eel bracelet slithered off her wrist and onto the floor. She clicked her fingers and ten, twenty, thirty eels emerged from the tank and wriggled toward her. There were so many, it looked like the ground was moving. It was a disgusting, stomach-turning sight. I felt like I might vomit, watching the way they swarmed around the hem of her dress.

"Watch her, my little chickens," she cooed. "I'll get the suit. And then you're getting in the water." She opened the door to her office and walked out.

I immediately ran over to the door, but the eels all raised themselves up and blocked it, each one of them writhing and hissing at me. They were so long, they covered the whole door and frame, and one of them had coiled itself around the handle. I reached for it—perhaps it was a harmless, nice eel—and, fangs drawn, it pounced for me. I pulled my hand away just in time.

"What did I ever do to you?" I grumbled, rubbing the spot it had tried to sink its teeth into.

Moving on, I ran around the office, desperately trying to find another way out. I banged on the windows, but none of the swimmers looked up, too focused on their training. And even if they did see me, how could they help? I doubted any of them would take a break from training and risk throwing away their Olympic dreams anyway.

I looked again at the disgusting eels covering my only escape. They had layered themselves on top of one another so that they formed a living door on top of a door. It vibrated with their movements.

What did I know about eels? I remembered Riley talking about them. Somewhere in between his *Did you know?* monologue on lizards and frogs, he had mentioned eels. But what had he said? And why hadn't I paid more attention?

You can hypnotize them? No, that was snakes.

What had Riley said?

Eels travel three thousand miles to breed, and then they die? Yes! I remembered Riley saying that. Interesting, but not helpful at this point.

What else had he said?

I stared at their awful beady eyes—all looking at me as if they were one multiheaded creature—trying to jog my memory. The eyes . . . Riley had said their eyes were sensitive to light. The eels didn't like light.

I took my phone out of my pocket and switched on the flashlight.

Running at them and waving my phone around like it

was a sword, I pointed it at the eel on the door handle, my hand getting close enough for the eel to bite it, but it reared back and then fell onto the floor. I kept going, pointing my phone like a laser at their eyes and lunging for the door handle. Clear of eels, it opened, and I ran through it, racing down the stairs. I didn't glance back to see if the eels were slithering after me or slow down when the receptionist shouted, "STOP!"

Once out on the street, I ducked into the first drugstore I came to. Then I ran straight back out because I felt singing bubbling up inside me as soon as the sound of the music playing over the store speakers hit my ears.

As I leaned against a bike rack, catching my breath, my legs were shaking. Part of me just wanted to go home and wait for Mom. But what if Mom couldn't help me? How would Mom know how to break a spell? I had to do it. And I couldn't just go home now, take a break, and then pick up my villain-visiting later. What if I got splashed with a puddle from a passing car? How long could I avoid water? And how long would it be until that NyQuil wore off and John broke out of Romy's house? No, I couldn't waste a moment. I had to keep going.

With shaking hands, I typed *Forever Young* into my phone. The address of the corporate headquarters was on Fifth Avenue, less than a mile away. According to the Forever Young website, the Evil Queen, or Elvira Queen, was listed as owner and CEO.

I took off running. This was my last shot. If the Evil Queen couldn't—or wouldn't—help me, John would stay a beast forever, and I'd have to spend the rest of my life avoiding water and music—which would make me a total weirdo, but still a lot less weird than being a mermaid.

I weaved in and out of the crowds as I ran, noticing people stopping to stare at me. Or more specifically, looking at my bald head. They probably wondered if I was sick. I really couldn't have cared less about my hair anymore. Being bald would be fine. There was so much more at stake now.

There was a security guard at the entrance of Forever Young. He did a double take when I approached, looking pointedly at my stained, sweat-soaked sweatshirt and bald head. I guessed I didn't look like the usual clients who strolled through the doors of Forever Young.

One of my mom's expressions popped into my head.

I'd always thought it was silly, but it seemed like it might be helpful now.

I threw back my shoulders, lifted up my chin, and made eye contact with the security guard while remembering Mom's words, that *self-confidence is the best outfit.* It worked—or maybe he just felt sorry for me. Either way, he opened the door and ushered me into a bright atrium that looked like a fancy health spa or clinic. The receptionist was even wearing a white lab coat. I approached her, and she looked at me with the same slightly disgusted expression the security guard had.

"I need to see Elvira Queen," I said, brainstorming some lies that might convince her to let me through.

But the receptionist just consulted something on her desk and then looked back at me.

"Yes," she said. "She's expecting you."

I didn't know if this was good, bad, or terrifying news.

"Thirty-fifth floor," said the receptionist. "Elevators are on the right."

By the time I stepped off the elevator on the thirty-fifth floor, I had rehearsed what I was going to say to the Evil

Queen thirty-five times. And then when I saw her, I forgot every word.

She was . . . magnificent. It seemed impossible that Snow White—who was, I knew from firsthand experience, spectacularly pretty—would ever come close to surpassing the queen's beauty.

The Evil Queen was standing with her back to me when I stepped out of the elevator into the big open space of the thirty-fifth floor. As she turned around to face me, she was holding a glass bottle that contained a greenish liquid in her gloved hands. She was dressed in an all-black, impeccably tailored dress and a cape that reached her knees. Her hair was pulled back from her face into a ponytail, accentuating her high cheekbones and grayish-violet eyes. Even though she had impossibly long black eyelashes, it seemed that the only makeup she was wearing was a deep red lipstick.

"I've been expecting you," she said.

I stared at her blankly.

"Don't look so frightened," she said.

But I *was* frightened. The Evil Queen was possibly even more evil than the Sea Witch. She had been so obsessed with envy over Snow White's beauty and youth—which made no sense because she was actually, as far as I could see, more beautiful than Snow White—that she'd told the huntsman to take her into the forest and kill her, and then she'd eaten what she'd believed to be Snow White's heart. So, basically, I was standing in front of a bloodthirsty wannabe cannibal.

"You shouldn't believe everything my stepdaughter says. Especially what she says about me."

Did she know that I had met Snow White?

The queen placed the bottle on a counter that ran along the length of one of the walls. The counter space was filled with other glass bottles that were bubbling over with colorful liquids, though I didn't see any burners or even wires that would explain where the heat was coming from.

Although there were floor-to-ceiling windows on one end of the thirty-fifth floor, the lighting was dim. There was a shimmer in the air and a hint of a scent of burnt apples.

"So, you and Snow White, you talk to each other?" I asked, wondering if they were on friendly terms and, if so, whether this was good or bad news for me.

"Oh no," she replied. "We don't talk. I'm far too busy for that. And we don't have the same interests anymore. I do like to keep an eye on her, though." She pointed at a wall that was filled with mirrors of all shapes and sizes. She walked toward a normal-sized one that had a gilded wooden frame around it.

"Go ahead, take a look," she said, ushering me over.

I looked into the mirror. Instead of seeing my reflection, I saw the room where Snow White and I had met. Snow White was pacing up and down, swishing her skirt in an agitated way and yelling at Shiny, who was standing in front of her, hands hanging by her side with the pouty expression of a kid getting in trouble. I could see them both and the room clearly, as if I were watching it all on TV. Their voices were faint, but I guessed that if I leaned into the mirror, I would be able to hear what they were saying.

"She's very upset about you," said the queen, peering into the mirror and gazing at Snow White, reminding me of the intense way Dad stared at paintings whenever we went to a museum. "She'd want to stop frowning and grimacing like that." She paused and looked at me in an almost mischievous way. "She'll get wrinkles."

"So, do you know why I'm here?" I asked, guessing that the queen had watched my exchange with Snow White in her cottage and knew that I was desperate to break a counterspell. "Can you break the counterspell?"

"Indeed, I do and I can," she said. "I was hoping you'd come visit me. You have exactly what I need."

I really didn't like the sound of that. What could I possibly have that the Evil Queen needed? But I left that question alone and focused on the good news. She knew how to break the counterspell. John, Romy, and I would be free of this fairy-tale nightmare.

"So will you break the spell?" I asked. I didn't want a repeat of what had just happened with the Sea Witch.

She walked over to the counter with the bottles and stood behind it, stretching out both arms, like a game show hostess displaying prizes on the wheel of fortune.

"I can and I will," she said. "If we can come to a mutually beneficial arrangement."

I gulped. Loudly.

"Now, don't be frightened," she said, picking up one of the bottles.

When you have been told not once but twice in a matter

of minutes to not be frightened, the effect is, well, pretty frightening. The more the queen told me not to be scared, the more reason I believed there was to be terrified.

"I know I—well, all of us 'villains'—have a bad reputation," she continued. "The princesses are always bad-mouthing us. And it's most unfair. There's really no basis to it. Take Cinderella's stepmother. She was just a single mother looking out for her daughters. And those girls really have their limitations. Not the sharpest knives in the drawer. Their mother had to do what she had to do."

She shrugged her shoulders.

I really didn't care about the villains' "bad reputations"—though from the way Lady Graff and the Sea Witch had acted when I'd met them, it seemed like they deserved them. I just wanted one of them to help me break a spell. But the Evil Queen was on a roll now—I was learning that these fairy-tale villains liked their speeches—and she kept going.

"And that Rapunzel! An out-of-control teenager, vaping, out till all hours, hanging out with a terrible crowd. Her stepmother was just being a responsible parent. Gothel had to ground that girl."

I resisted the urge to point out that turning Rapunzel into a shut-in was not the same as "grounding" someone.

"And look at the Sea Witch," she said. "The Little Mermaid didn't even try to negotiate—she couldn't wait to trade in her tail—and the Sea Witch gets the blame for not making a fair deal.

"You really shouldn't pay any attention to what the princesses say. They are fools. They haven't evolved one bit. This world is wasted on them. There are so many opportunities for wealth and power." She paused and gazed down at her bottles, then over at the mirrors. "I'm building an empire. I'll be the richest woman in the world. And what do they do? Keep their sights so low. Still waiting for their princes to rescue them. The only one doing anything remotely interesting is Belle. At least she's not obsessed with finding a husband.

"No, I'm the one you want to do business with," said the queen. "Now, how old are you?"

She gave me the same examining look she had given Snow White in the mirror.

"Thirteen," I answered.

"Very good. Well, your payment won't be apparent for another seven years."

"Payment?" I had hardly any money—just the fifty dollars my grandparents had sent me for my birthday. But I had a horrible feeling that that wasn't what the Evil Queen was talking about.

"You didn't think I'd do it for free? What kind of business do you think this is?"

I had no idea what kind of business she was running. Was it a spell depot or a skin care company or a spying operation?

"What kind of payment?" I gulped, thinking again about how she had once ordered her huntsman to bring her back Snow White's heart. What if she expected me to kill someone? There was no way I was doing that.

"Ten years," she answered, shaking one of the bottles so that the liquid in it swirled from purple to yellow to black.

"Ten years of what?" I gasped, relieved that she wasn't considering me as a possible assassin. (I'd gotten a bit carried away there.) But what did she mean? Was she expecting me to sign up for a Cinderella-type setup and wear rags and clean up her office/lab for the next ten years?

"Your youth," said the queen, placing a stopper on the bottle she'd been holding. "Youth willingly given is so much easier to use—a much better ingredient than youth taken by force—so that's your payment."

My youth? What was she talking about?

"I'll take the ten years from twenty to thirty."

Chapter 24

MY TWENTIES. I'D BEEN SORT OF LOOKING forward to that decade in a general, unspecified way. From what I'd heard and seen (mostly from watching *Friends*), it would be all about going to college, having roommates, getting a job, wearing cute clothes, traveling, and having fun before the real business of working, and even possibly having a baby, would start. (That last bit was obviously the furthest thing from my mind, but I knew it was something most people did at some point.)

How could I give up my twenties?

"Just your dewy complexion," said the queen, as if reading my mind. "You can live your life however you want, but I will take those ten years of plump cheeks and smooth forehead and big eyes."

"So, I'll wake up twenty, but I'll look thirty?" I asked, beginning to understand, and not liking her offer one bit.

"Exactly," said the queen.

Could I bargain? Was that an option? "How about if I gave you fifty to sixty instead?" I asked.

The queen laughed. I guessed that was a no.

"You'd better decide quickly," she said, pointing at my legs with a glass dropper she was holding between two fingers. "Ticktock."

So, my choice was between premature aging or being a mermaid.

It wasn't just about looking thirty at twenty. After that, I'd be thirty and look forty, and then be fifty and look sixty, and so on, until I was the wrinkliest old lady in my bridge club.

But I knew what I had to do. It wasn't just about me and taking drastic, socially devastating steps to stop sprouting a fish tail. It was also about John and the hulking, hairy, monstrous form he'd be forced to inhabit forever. And making sure that there were no more traumatic incidents at my school. What was to stop Cinderella from sending more flocks of attacking birds? Snow White might deploy Shiny and her crew to kidnap Romy or Riley or anyone I cared about. And I didn't even want to think about what Rapunzel could do with all her extra hair. Tie people up?

"Okay," I whispered. "Take them."

"Excellent," she said, all business. "I'll use it to fuel my newest line of skin care products, Essence of Youth. You could even use it yourself. It will be *the* miracle cream."

She laughed, clearly amused at the ironic possibility of me needing—and having to pay for—an antiaging cream that I would, in a way, create.

"Although at five hundred dollars an ounce," she said, taking in my beat-up sneakers and tattered jeans, "I don't think you are my target customer."

She continued working at the counter, using the dropper to extract minute amounts of solutions from different bottles. She then mixed the different liquids together in a thumb-sized silver bottle. I took in the rest of the office while she worked. One wall was covered in floor-to-ceiling shelves, all of them filled with books. There was quite an eclectic mix of titles. I was able to make out some of them: *How to Win Friends and Influence People*, *The Art of the Deal*, *Look Younger This Time Next Year*, *Advanced Potion-Making*, and—I rubbed my eyes when I saw it because I couldn't believe the queen had it—one of my mom's books.

"But women—men, too, they're getting more and more susceptible to all this—will find a way to get the money when they see what my products can do," continued the Evil Queen. "They're going to get very motivated when they look in the mirrors." She gestured over at the wall of mirrors. "Go on. You can see for yourself. Look at the two in the center."

I shuffled over to the two largest mirrors in the middle of the wall. The words TAKE A LOOK AT TOMORROW were inscribed on the glass of the first mirror. I wasn't even sure it was a mirror. I stood right in front of it, but my reflection did not appear in it, just those words, TAKE A LOOK AT TOMORROW. The mirror alongside it was identical, except that the words inscribed on it were a little different: TAKE A LOOK AT TOMORROW WITH FOREVER YOUNG. It, too, didn't show my reflection.

"Turn the dial underneath," said the queen.

Just below the bottom of the frames of both mirrors, there were identical dials that marked out numbers in increments of ten. One click to the right would move it to ten, two clicks would take it up to twenty, and so on until one hundred.

I turned the dial underneath the first mirror, noticing that my reflection was beginning to appear in front of me. I glanced up and then looked over my shoulder, looking for the person in the mirror because the girl in the mirror wasn't me. But then I blinked, and the girl in the mirror blinked back. I shook my head, and she shook her head. I lifted a hand and waved. She lifted a hand and waved back at me.

She had big, hazel-colored eyes (again, just like me), a sprinkling of freckles on her cheeks, a sweep of dark bangs across her forehead, and—this really surprised me because I hadn't even gotten my ears pierced yet—a tiny gold stud in her nose. She looked friendly and pretty and cooler than I ever thought I'd be. But it was me. I glanced back down at the dial and saw that I had turned it to the second marker. I was looking at myself seven years from now. This is what I would look like at age twenty.

"Keep going," said the queen in a soothing voice. "You can see it all in that mirror . . . thirty, forty, fifty. Keep going."

I reached out to the dial but then dropped my hand and stepped away from the mirror. This wasn't right. We weren't supposed to see into the future like this. I looked again at the inscription on the other mirror, TAKE A LOOK AT TOMORROW WITH FOREVER YOUNG, and with a sickening feeling I understood that the queen had developed the most powerful advertisement imaginable for her products. Stand in front of mirror one, and you would see how you would look at age forty without the Forever Young products—presumably a bit wrinkly and saggy and, well, old. And then you'd stand in front of mirror two and turn the dial to forty again, and you'd see a different, wrinkle-free, youthful you. And you could have what mirror two showed you; all you had to do was pay five hundred dollars an ounce for the queen's cream. And how long would an ounce last? It was a tiny amount. Maybe a couple of weeks? The queen would make a fortune. Even a woman like my mom—who liked to say *there's nothing wrong with looking your age*—would have a hard time saying no to the Forever Young products if she got a look at herself in mirror two.

"Are these in your stores?" I asked, imagining lines of people waiting to get their turn in front of the awful mirrors. They should come with a big warning underneath. DANGER: THESE MIRRORS WILL MAKE YOU MISERABLE.

"Not yet," said the queen. "I needed a crucial ingredient for the Essence of Youth serum. Without that I can't make what mirror two promises. But now I can. You, child, are the crucial ingredient."

I felt like I was going to be sick. My choice wasn't premature aging or mermaid tail/condemn John to life as a beast. My choice was premature aging and inflicting those dreadful mirrors on the world or mermaid tail/ condemn John to life as a beast. If I cooperated with the Evil Queen, I'd be helping to push the awful *look perfect, aim for unattainable beauty* ideal that was being forced on all of us. I thought of the girls in my grade, practically weeping in the restroom when they had a few zits—and, if I was honest, I'd been one of those girls too—and now I was going to make it even worse for all of us. I'd be helping to bring forth enchanted mirrors that would show people that if they just bought the right products and followed the right regimen, they really could be "Forever Young." It would take the looks obsession to a whole new, terrifying level. Would mothers start looking younger than their daughters?

Weren't there lots of Greek myths about the perils of vanity and curiosity and the search for eternal youth? Those never ended well. Didn't everyone know those stories? Maybe people would feel the same fear and unease I was feeling and choose not to turn the dials. Maybe people would do the right thing. I hoped so. Would I be to blame if I gave her what she needed to inflict this on the world? But if I didn't do it, John would be a beast for the rest of his life. How could I do that to him and his parents? I had to do what I came here to do. I had to break the counterspell.

"Is it ready?" I asked the queen.

"Yes," she said, lifting up the tiny silver bottle and pouring out the contents. The liquid transformed into a silver-colored hard candy before it hit the table.

"Do I just eat it?" I asked, taking if off the table.

"Not yet," said the queen. "The timing is crucial."

She walked over to the bookshelves and pulled out a book.

It was called *Urban Myths and Fables: A Forensic Examination*. It was another book that my mom had written, another book that I'd never read. As soon as I got out of this mess, if I ever got out of this mess, I was going to read them all.

The queen flipped through the pages.

"You need to take the spell-breaker at precisely 6:06 p.m. Not a moment before, not a moment later. There's a Manhattan Solstice this evening," she said.

Manhattan Solstice. I'd heard about that. It was when the sun lined up just exactly with the street grid of Manhattan. Had Mom written about it in that book? What else was in there?

I glanced at my phone. I had about an hour before I could take it. Surely John would stay asleep for another sixty minutes, right? And I could stay away from water and music for that long. Couldn't I?

I put the spell-breaker in my back pocket and set an alarm on my phone for 6:05 p.m.

So I had the counterspell-breaking candy, and soon

I'd be able to end this nightmare. Now I needed to deliver on my end of the bargain. "I'm ready to do my . . . part of the deal."

"You can go," said the queen. "You gave me what I needed when you looked in the mirror. But you won't notice anything until you wake on the morning of your twentieth birthday."

So, that was something to look forward to.

My phone buzzed in my back pocket. I took it out. I didn't recognize the number that popped up on the screen. But once I read the message, I knew who it was from.

Turn yourself in. Or your little brother gets it.

Chapter 25

SNOW WHITE.

I ran out of Elvira Queen's office into the elevator and called the number that had sent the text. No one answered.

Running out of the headquarters, I called Dad.

"Cia!" he shouted. "Where are you? What is going on? You need to come home right now!"

"Dad," I said, ignoring him. "Where is Riley? Is Riley with you?"

"What?" said Dad, his tone changing from angry to worried. "Riley's at a birthday party. . . ."

"What party?" I shouted. "Where is the party?"

"Central Park Zoo," said Dad. "Cia—"

"Dad, Riley's in danger. You need to get to Central Park now."

My phone pinged.

"Dad, I gotta go!" I shouted, turning and running in the opposite direction, toward the park. "You need to come now! Call the police!" I didn't know what Snow White was planning, but I was going to use everything I could to stop her.

I looked at the text message that had just come through and immediately stopped running. It was a photo of a very happy-looking Riley standing beside an equally happy-looking Alice Oberle, a cute princess/unicorn-obsessed girl in his class. Alice was wearing a Cinderella costume and a sash that said BIRTHDAY PRINCESS. Standing on either side of the two kindergartners were Cinderella and Snow White.

My Snow White.

I couldn't tell if the Cinderella was the same one who had assaulted that kid at the birthday party that had made the news. It seemed from the angle of the photo that Snow

White had taken the group selfie. At the edge of the photo, I saw Shiny and Speckless looking over at the group. I studied the picture more closely and saw that they were standing next to the penguin enclosure.

I'm on my way. And I can break the spell, I texted back. **DON'T HURT MY BROTHER.**

I paused, one hand hovering over my phone, my mind running through a list of possible *or elses*.

Or else I'll tell everyone you're a homicidal fairy-tale nightmare and no one will ever want to marry you.

Or else I'll kill you.

I didn't really mean that last one. But I was angry! I couldn't remember ever being so mad. How dare Snow White use my little brother as a bargaining chip in her pointless quest for a rich husband! For a marriage that would last—what?—a day? Riley didn't have anything to do with any of this. He was just a little kid. My little brother. I felt sick with fear. Snow White had been ready to kill me. What was she going to do with my brother?

But I knew how to break the spell. As long as I got to her in time, everything would be okay.

I pushed my phone back into my pocket and started

running again, not stopping until I got to the entrance of the zoo and joined the end of the line. I doubled over to try to catch my breath and used the edge of my sweatshirt to wipe off the sweat that was streaming down my face.

But the line was taking too long, and I didn't have a ticket. There was a large group—a family with a couple of teenagers and a few little kids pushing their own strollers—going through the entrance, and I grabbed my chance. I put my head down and slipped in with them.

Once inside, I checked the signposts and ran for the Polar Circle. The zoo was packed with families out for a Friday afternoon, and I weaved in between strollers and clusters of little kids rooted to the spot, gazing excitedly at the snow monkeys and grizzly bears.

I'd finally made it to the penguins when I saw Rapunzel, her long braid slung over one shoulder. So Snow White had called in reinforcements. I scanned the crowd, wondering if the Little Mermaid and Belle were close by too. Rapunzel was sitting on a bench, the fabric of her purple dress spilling over onto the seat beside her. She was sucking on the straw of her soda can. I ran up to her.

"Where's Snow White?" I said through gritted teeth.

She stared at me. "Do I know you?"

"I need to see her. Now." I clenched my fists and leaned in menacingly.

"Riiight," she said slowly, getting up from the bench and throwing her drink in the trash. "I'm going to go now."

As she walked away, I saw she was wearing sneakers underneath her dress. I looked at her more closely. The straw-colored mass of hair was a wig, with some brown strands poking out around the hairline, and she had a sprinkling of acne on her forehead. The real, likely evil Rapunzel would have had flawless skin. This one was obviously just hired to act as Rapunzel for kids' birthday parties.

"Um, sorry," I muttered. "I thought you were someone else."

I took off again, resolving to ignore any other princess look-alikes until I was sure I was dealing with the real thing.

I didn't have to wait long.

I came upon Snow White in front of the sea lion enclosure. There was a mob of kindergarten girls around her and a handful of starstruck little boys standing off to the side, throwing adoring glances at her. I couldn't blame them. She did *seem* adorable. It was hard to believe that this was the same woman who had masterminded my kidnapping and attempted murder. Snow White knelt down to tie a girl's shoelaces, pulled out a handkerchief for another who had the sniffles, and opened a juice box for a boy, all the while smiling and whistling. The children loved it and skipped along beside her, their faces beaming joyful smiles. I came up to them and saw Snow White—pointing at a sea lion through the glass wall that surrounded the enclosure—regaling them with a story about the antics of a naughty sea lion called Cecil. The children collapsed into fits of giggles.

I searched the crowd for Riley, recognizing lots of the faces of his classmates. My heart dropped as I realized that he was not among them. Trying not to scare the kids, I walked up to Snow White, smiling at her fans, and grabbed her shoulder.

"Where is my brother?" I whispered into her ear.

Snow White looked down at the children.

"I have a prize for whoever can tell me how many penguins there are!" she said in a singsong voice, pointing over at the penguin enclosure.

The children ran toward the penguin enclosure screaming with excitement.

She turned to me, the smile falling from her face as if she had pulled off a mask.

"Where is my brother?" I repeated, starting to feel scared now. You couldn't leave a little kid on their own in a place as huge and crowded as the Central Park Zoo.

"He's fine," she said, pointing toward the sea lions. "For now."

I looked over at the big animals sprawled out on the rocks around their pool, basking in the afternoon sunlight. Some of them were swimming in the water, their sleek heads bobbing up and down comically. I saw the opening of a cave, just partially visible in the long shadows of the afternoon. Riley was sitting on a rock at the entrance, flanked by Shiny and Speckless.

"Riley," I gasped.

"He's fine," said Snow White impatiently. "He thinks he's going to feed the sea lions."

I looked at him again. He wasn't fine. I couldn't see his face clearly. But I could tell from the way he was sitting, hunched over with his hands balled into tight fists, that he was nervous. Being that close to water without wearing a floaty would make him terrified, and just looking at the water made me feel really uncomfortable too.

"Listen, I can break the spell. Just let him go," I said, reaching for my phone. It was 6:02 p.m.

"Then do it," said Snow White. "And I'll tell Shiny and Speckless to bring him over here."

"You just have to wait four minutes." I swallowed. My mouth was so dry, I was having difficulty speaking. I got the spell-breaking candy from my pocket and held it out to Snow White. "Look, when I eat this, the spell will be broken. Please, just get Riley out of there now. Get him away from the water."

There was a roar from somewhere behind me.

I turned and saw a furious woman approaching us.

It was the Sea Witch.

She charged at me and Snow White.

"You don't walk away from a deal with me," she hissed.

Her dress flapping around her, she barged in between me and Snow White and grabbed both of my arms, and the candy I'd been holding went flying to the ground.

"Get it!" I shouted to Snow White.

A snake or sea serpent came out from beneath the Sea Witch's skirts and slithered toward the candy just as Snow White lunged at it.

Snow White and I both screamed. Every kid near the penguin enclosure turned around to look and then started stampeding toward us.

"It's the Evil Queen!" yelled a girl, who clearly didn't know her fairy-tale villains very well. She wore the yellow ball gown of a Disney Belle, which she yanked up around her knees as she charged in our direction, her legs pumping like crazy.

"This party is awesome!" screamed a little boy from Riley's tae kwon do class who was dressed up like a medieval knight. Snow White was sprawled on the ground, one hand out searching for the candy, the other whacking a sea serpent with her slipper.

"I can't find it!" she screamed.

I tried to wriggle out of the Sea Witch's grip, but she had me pinned to her so tightly, I could smell her revolting breath. Old fish and rotten seaweed. Craning my neck, I looked into the sea lion enclosure and saw Riley standing up on the rock and looking at the

Snow-White-and-sea-serpent scuffle. He shouted out my name. He sounded terrified.

"Riley," I gasped, trying not to gag on the stench wafting from the Sea Witch's mouth.

As the Sea Witch cackled and Snow White continued to yell, a mob of kindergartners descended on us.

"Find the candy!" Snow White shouted at them. The kids skidded to a stop, got down on their hands and knees, and joined Snow White on the ground.

Riley's little knight friend, still holding his sword aloft, went straight for me and the Sea Witch.

"You let her go!" he shouted, brandishing his sword in her face.

"Stupid boy," spat the Sea Witch. "Be gone."

The sky started to darken, and there was a rumble of distant thunder followed by a flash of lightning. Hail began to fall, the icy lumps pelting the ground so quickly that within seconds there was a covering of shiny whiteness on my jeans and sneakers.

The children screamed and ran for cover, abandoning Snow White and their treasure hunt. Riley's friend, though, using his shield as an umbrella, stood his ground and kept demanding my release. Whatever they were teaching those kids at tae kwon do, it was good stuff.

"Got it!" yelled Snow White, getting to her feet, clutching the candy.

I heard my phone beeping. It was the alarm. It was 6:05 p.m.

"Give it to me!" I screamed, watching the sea serpent recoil its head as if getting ready to bite Snow White's ankle.

"No!" shouted the Sea Witch, letting me go so suddenly that I fell onto the ground. I looked over at Snow White and saw the candy, propelled by water shooting out of a ring on the Sea Witch's hand, make its way from the tips of Snow White's fingers over the wall and into the sea lion enclosure, where it landed in the mouth of a very whiskery sea lion, who swallowed it, snorted, and then dove into the water.

The Sea Witch laughed and raised both hands, shaking her fists at the sky. The air crackled with electricity, and then as lightning flashed, sheets of hail began to fall so heavily and so fast that I could scarcely see in front of me.

"No!" I screamed. My only chance of breaking the

spell was now inside a sea lion. Snow White screamed too, looking ready for murder. Now that the candy was gone, would she revert to plan A? Taking me, or my brother, down if I didn't cooperate?

Riley. Riley!

Where was Riley?

I hauled myself up to my feet and turned, looking over the wall into the sea lion enclosure, holding my hand above my eyes so that I could make out my brother in the middle of the hailstorm. It looked like a typhoon had touched down onto the pool. The water was churning and heaving, and waves crashed against the glass walls with such force that I was covered in salty spray. Even the sea lions that hadn't taken shelter in the cave were having difficulty navigating the choppy waters, pushing furiously against a current that was pulling them down.

Riley saw me, waved frantically, and ran toward the edge of the water. I couldn't hear him, but I saw him mouth, "Cia!" He was getting dangerously close to the waves. I yelled out for him to stop.

"Stay where you are, Riley!" I screamed, but he couldn't hear me over the sounds of the hail and the wind. He kept going, stumbled, and then for a heart-stopping moment he teetered near the edge.

Then he fell.

His blond head was visible on the surface for just a second, and then it was gone.

"RILEY!" I screamed.

Somewhere in the recesses of my brain, the information I'd learned in science about the respiratory system surfaced. I remembered that an average person has thirty to sixty seconds to run out of air once they go underwater. Thirty to sixty seconds before they unintentionally breathe in water. Thirty to sixty seconds before drowning begins. About two minutes before they die. Riley had less than two minutes before his lungs filled with water. I needed to save him. I needed to save my brother. I knew what would happen once my legs touched that water, but I didn't care. All that mattered was Riley.

"RILEY!" I screamed again.

I tried to scramble over the wall to get to him, grabbing the edge with both hands and pulling myself up, but as soon as I got some traction, my hands slipped, and I fell to the ground. I yelled for help, screaming that my brother was drowning as I tried again to clear the wall. I felt myself being lifted up and saw, out of the corner of my eye, that it was Snow White, grunting with effort, who gave me the push that I needed. I'd wonder later why she had helped me. Did she just realize that she needed to help a child whom she'd put in danger, or did she know something about the way the magic worked that I didn't understand?

I tumbled over the wall and fell heavily onto the stone surrounding the pool. Staring at the spot that I had last seen Riley before he disappeared under the waves, I raised my arms and dove in. As soon as I touched the water, it began to happen. I felt my sneakers being pulled from my feet by some unknown force, and I didn't care. I felt my legs fusing together, and I didn't care. I felt a tremendous surge of power where my legs had been, and I didn't care. All I cared about was Riley. Nothing else mattered. Only Riley. I pushed through the water, my massive tail propelling me down into the black depths, slicing effortlessly through the current.

I saw Riley kicking his legs and moving his arms like he was swimming through mud, trying desperately to get back up to the surface. His limbs gave out just as I swooped down and picked him up and carried his exhausted body away from the murky bottom.

I lifted Riley onto the rocks that bordered the pool and heaved myself up beside him, scooting backward so that my tail wouldn't hit him and inadvertently push him back into the water. He was soaked and limp in my arms, and I shook him by his shoulders, then held him against my chest, thumping his back with the palm of my hand. I screamed for help, shouting through the blizzard of hail that was still falling all around me. I kept thumping and squeezing and screaming, furious at the now-useless tail that kept me rooted to the spot. I wanted to carry my brother and run with him to a hospital. To someone who could save him.

I felt Riley shudder in my arms. Then he began to cough. It was, I thought, the most wonderful sound I had ever heard. My eyes filled with tears, and I sobbed with relief.

"Riley," I gasped, his name catching in my throat. "Riley, it's okay."

He coughed again and grabbed his neck, his eyes wide with pain and fright.

"You're okay," I said. "I've got you." He was shivering, and his teeth had started chattering. I pulled him closer to me. He felt so skinny, and I could feel the hammering of his heartbeat vibrating against my chest. But he was breathing. He was alive.

The hail slowed, then stopped altogether, and I saw a police officer running toward us, his belly wobbling from side to side. For a fraction of a second I thought about diving back into the water. How could I explain this six-foot-long tail? I was both disgusted and amazed by it. It was beautiful; threads of dark denim blue—it was as if my jeans had become part of the tail—were woven through the green scales that were arranged in a scalloped pattern that got smaller and more delicate as it reached the end. And it seemed to be affecting my mind, too, because I felt drawn to the water. I watched the sea lions shuffle awkwardly to the edge and then slide back in, gliding into the pool without making a splash. I wanted to join them. But even if I did dive in, how long could I hide out in the sea lion enclosure in the Central Park Zoo? Panic cut through the relief coursing through me. What would my life be like now that I was a mermaid?

I felt Riley's arms tighten around me, and he pressed his head against my shoulder. I knew that I couldn't leave him. Not now. Not ever. If I had to live the rest of my life as a mermaid—and it seemed that I would—then that was okay, because Riley might have died if I hadn't grown this tail. Becoming a mermaid and not losing my little brother was a fair trade. No doubt about it. I knew that I would do it all again if I had to.

"Cia," he said, his voice barely a whisper. "You saved me."

Chapter 26

EVERYONE ALL RIGHT OVER HERE?" SAID THE police officer, wheezing a little from running so fast and scrambling over the enclosure wall. "Paramedics are on the way. We'll get you both taken care of in no time."

He got down on his knees so that he was eye level with Riley and me.

"I'm Officer Rodriguez," he said. "How about you two?"

"Riley and Cia," I answered, adjusting my position on the rocks. Riley was starting to feel heavy.

"Hey, Riley," said Officer Rodriguez, smiling. "What's black and white and goes round and round?"

Riley turned his head to look at him.

"A penguin in a revolving door," said Officer Rodriguez, without missing a beat. "What do penguins like to eat?" he continued, gently lifting Riley's wrist and placing his thumb on the inside. "Brrrrrrrrritos."

Riley let out a little laugh, and I decided that I loved Officer Rodriguez and his corny jokes.

I leaned back on my arms and lifted my face toward the sun. The storm had passed, and I could hear the hum of the crowd on the other side of the enclosure as people resumed their Friday afternoon outings.

I closed my eyes and shook my head, enjoying the feeling of my hair brushing against my cheeks. It had returned at just about the same time as my tail had disappeared. Just after Riley said that I had saved him.

The ambulance took Riley and me to Lenox Hill Hospital. We were brought to a room, and while a doctor was examining us, Dad burst in.

"RILEY! CIA!"

"We're okay, Dad," I said, lifting myself up from the bed I was lying on.

"I just . . . ," gasped Dad, sitting on the bed so hard that it made me jump. "They told me what happened. . . . You almost drowned?" His eyes darted from me to Riley and then back to me. "Are they okay?" he asked the doctor.

"They're fine," she said, taking a step back. "Just need a good night's sleep and maybe a quiet day tomorrow."

I smiled. I was really looking forward to a good night's sleep.

Dad put one arm around me, reached across the gap between the beds, and wrapped the other arm around Riley.

"This doesn't work," he said, getting up and pushing the beds together. Riley laughed and snuggled in beside me.

I scooched over, and Dad sat down next to me, swinging his legs up onto the bed. Dad didn't ask me about the phone call we'd had just before I ran to the zoo, and I hoped I'd never have to explain to him how I knew Riley had been in danger. Dad seemed so relieved and happy to see Riley and me; maybe his memory of the call would get wiped out along with all his worries.

"CIA! RILEY!"

Mom burst into the room and threw her purse on the

floor, running over to the beds to squeeze Riley and me in a hug. I breathed in honey and peaches, the fragrance of the perfume she always wore. She held us so tightly that I could feel her heart hammering. My mom was back. The fight over the poster didn't matter anymore. The fact that she had taken me to Madame Fredepia as a baby—that didn't matter either. She was back.

"Mom, you're squishing me," said Riley, squirming a little.

"Don't care," said Mom. But she pulled back and covered his face with kisses.

Then she turned to me and held my face in her hands. I closed my eyes for a moment, relishing the feeling of relief that my mother was here.

I opened my eyes.

"My beautiful girl," she said, her eyes brimming with tears. "What you have been through . . ."

I didn't know if she meant almost drowning at the Central Park Zoo or my too-close encounters with magic and fairy-tale characters.

But it didn't matter. Mom was home.

"Scoot over," she said to Riley, sitting down beside

him on the bed. She squeezed in, and all four of us lay together on the two beds. Me and Riley in the middle, Mom and Dad flanking us on either side.

Mom and Dad wrapped their arms around us and then stretched over and held each other's hands. No one spoke. I felt perfectly happy and warm and safe, as if I could have stayed in those hospital beds forever.

"Enough of this love snuggle," said Riley, beginning to wriggle beside me.

It was time to go home.

While Dad was upstairs getting Riley ready for bed, Mom and I sat at the kitchen table finishing the grilled cheese sandwiches Dad had made and sipping on mugs of hot chocolate. I'd caught her up on the events of the last three days.

"Cia, I'm so sorry," she said. "I had no idea Madame Fredepia would cause so much trouble."

"But you knew she could cast spells?" I asked. I was dying to know if, when she went to visit Madame Fredepia all those years ago, Mom suspected that she had been visiting a fairy godmother, not just a baby sleep-whisperer.

"Well . . ." Mom sighed. "She did seem to have expertise in that area, and I thought, why not try? I really was worn out from not sleeping. . . ."

"So, you believed—I mean, you believe—in magic, Mom?"

"Of course I do." She shrugged as if admitting to a belief in magic was no big deal. Like it was a completely normal thing.

"But . . . but . . . ," I sputtered. "Why did you never tell me . . . that . . . that . . . magic is real?"

"Well," said Mom, pausing to take a long drink of her hot chocolate, "I really didn't see the need. You need to focus on schoolwork, and believing in magic would just be a distraction. I mean, how does knowing magic is real actually help you?"

Would knowing magic was real have distracted me from schoolwork? Definitely. And would knowing magic was real have helped me? I didn't know about that. Even without having the inside scoop, I'd managed to find out about the counterspell and break it. But how could she not have told me? This just seemed like something you should tell your child about. Maybe not Riley, but I was a teenager.

"Look, it's not like I needed to tell you, Cia," said Mom, smiling, as if reading my mind. "You know you can't actually do magic."

I'd never thought I could *do* magic, and I was about to say so, but then something occurred to me. In the past three days, I'd found out there were fairy-tale characters living among us, some of whom were dispensing spells. What else was going on?

"Mom, what else do I not know about?"

When her baby wouldn't sleep, Mom had consulted a fairy godmother. The Evil Queen had one of her books. Mom had tried—for most of my childhood—to warn me away from fairy-tale princesses. And as a professor of mythology and folklore, she spent months every year traveling to remote places researching stories. What else did she know about? What else was Mom not telling me?

"Cia," Mom said, reaching across the table and placing her hand on top of mine, "of course there are things you don't know. But you shouldn't know them yet. Knowing them now, it would be dangerous."

"Mom, c'mon. I've negotiated with the Sea Witch. I've even *wrestled* with the Sea Witch! I struck a deal with the Evil Queen." I needed to talk to Mom about that later. Would I still have to give my youthful twenties to the queen even if I hadn't used the candy? I wasn't quite ready to think about that yet. "I figured out how to get into a restricted area in a hospital. I survived a pigeon attack—"

"You did," interrupted Mom, squeezing my hand. "But knowing more now . . . would be dangerous for you. And for Riley."

Riley.

I couldn't—I wouldn't do anything that might put Riley in danger. He had almost drowned because of the counterspell. There was a lot I didn't know about magic, but I knew one thing for sure. It *was* dangerous.

"Fine, Mom." I sighed. "Then can you just tell me why my tail disappeared? It just vanished when I was sitting on the rocks, but the sea lion ate the candy. How was the spell broken?"

"Ah," said Mom. She leaned back in her chair and smiled broadly. "*You* broke it, Cia. The abandonment of self leads to salvation."

"Abandonment of self?" Mom sounded like she was

talking to a class of her graduate students. "What does that mean?"

"It just means that love conquers all. You loved Riley more than you loved your legs." She paused and laughed. "Cia, you loved Riley more than you loved yourself. In the world of fairy tales, that's a game changer. That reboots everything."

"So, the tail won't come back?" I asked, looking down at my legs.

"No, no, it won't," said Mom. "The story's been told. It's all over." She held her mug out to me, and we clinked our cups in a toast.

"Mom, I gotta go to bed," I said, a wave of exhaustion hitting me so hard that I knew if I didn't get up immediately, I'd fall asleep at the table.

"Good night, sweetheart," said Mom. "I'm so proud of you."

"Thanks, Mom."

I was kind of proud of me too.

I walked upstairs and went into my bedroom, where I got into my pajamas and threw my clothes into a corner of my room. Tomorrow I would throw out the stained,

sweat-soaked sweatshirt and the jeans that had transformed into a fish tail and then back into jeans. I was
never going to wear them again.

I lay down on my bed, and it had never felt so comfy
and welcoming. I could barely keep my eyes open, but
there was one last thing I needed to do. I reached for my
phone and scrolled through the text messages that Romy
had sent—and that I so far had only had the chance to
glance at—while I was at the zoo and then at the hospital.
I found the one she had sent at 6:30 p.m., right around the
time Riley and I were lying on the rocks beside the sea
lion pool.

John's back!

It was followed by a line of smiley-face emojis.

I took a selfie of me lying back on my bed, my hair
fanning out over the entire pillow.

So am I, I texted back.

And then I slept.

Epilogue

AFTER THAT THINGS WENT BACK TO NORMAL.
Sort of.

Roger Wu's "sense of humor" doesn't really annoy me anymore. Probably because I suspect that I might actually be strong—taking on a diabolical villains and rescuing a little brother can give a girl some confidence—so whenever he yells out, "Cia, you are strong and powerful!" I say, "Thanks for the compliment," and his face drops. (And Mom's stopped leaving those notes in my bag, so he doesn't have any new material to work with.) My grades have slipped back to their usual just-above-average status, as I don't have hours to spend every night double-checking my homework. And we got a new science teacher. Mrs. Taylor never came back to Hill Country Middle School, instead choosing to open a bed-and-breakfast in upstate New York. Mrs. Stasevich, when she realized the stunning performance I had given her was a one-off and that I couldn't carry a tune, threw me out of choir class. I couldn't blame her. So, now I'm in Mr. Wilder's class preparing for some apocalyptic future when we have to live without electricity and clothing stores.

I decided that I did want to be part of the *Romeo and Juliet* production after all. I'm not getting to play the nurse, though. In a stroke of casting genius, Mrs. Stuart gave the role to Raul, and he's brilliant at it. But I'm still having a great time. Mrs. Stuart made me Raul's understudy, and I'm working on the costumes, putting together something gorgeous for Romy, who's playing Juliet.

A couple of weeks after things got back to normal, I asked Romy how she felt about the fact that most of the fairy-tale princesses were white. It felt weird to ask, and Romy laughed and told me to chill out. But later on, she texted me that she thought it was cool that I'd asked her.

It's not like we're having any deep and meaningful conversations or anything, but I feel like if we needed to have them, maybe we could.

I haven't seen much of John, and I'm worried that he might be avoiding me, which would be understandable. I turned him into a beast not once, but twice, and then used him to take down a mob of enchanted cleaning ladies. Given the circumstances, I wouldn't be dying to hang out with me either.

The Noah Agarwal/Hildee get-together was excruciatingly awful. Noah, who had obviously had no idea that Hildee was getting ready to print their wedding invitations (Romy and I had told him that Hildee just wanted to talk to him about New York University), didn't know how to react to the giggling, hair-twirling girl in front of him who seemed to have lost the power of speech. Hildee asked me to come along to the meeting, and I think she expected me to act as a matchmaker/conversation facilitator, which was so difficult that I started to feel sorry for Lady Graff and had a new appreciation for the challenges she faced getting her daughters—I assumed Wilhemina would be as tongue-tied and awkward as Hildee—a couple of marriage proposals. Even though Hildee barely said two words during the Noah get-together, she was delighted and grateful, and I was relieved that I had taken care of my side of our deal, though I felt bad about setting her up on a "date" when "dating" and trying to track down eligible bachelors was exactly what Hildee needed to stop doing. The next day I dropped off a gift at her house. The *Six Exceptional Kids Who Are Changing the World* book. I hoped it would give her some ideas.

Whenever my parents left the *New York Times* lying around, I checked out the wedding section, wondering if I'd see something about Snow White. I never did. Then one evening as my grade was wrapping up a field trip in the city and coming down the steps of the American Museum of Natural History, I saw her stepping out of a limousine. I caught a glimpse of the shortish driver in the front seat and wondered if it was one of the dwarfs returned to his proper size. A short, fat, bald man in a tuxedo helped Snow White out of the car, kissing her hand—on which she wore an enormous canary-yellow diamond—as she exited.

"That's Randall Fenton the fifth," said our new science

teacher. "Rolling in money . . . Gives a lot to the museum."

"That's Snow White," I said under my breath.

As she passed, she looked at me and smiled. She looked happy and exactly like the fairy-tale princess she was.

Shortly after Riley and I left the Central Park Zoo, the Sea Witch was arrested. By the FBI. A couple of agents—who had followed her to the park from the swimming academy—charged her with race fixing and the illicit drugging of swimmers. It turned out that some of the swimmers at her academy had been working with the FBI for over a year because, as one of them said, speaking anonymously to a reporter, "that woman should be behind bars."

I couldn't agree more.

It wasn't hard to keep track of Snow White's step-mother. She and her company, Forever Young, were making international headlines. A few weeks after the incident in the Central Park Zoo, the see-the-future mirrors were placed in all her stores, but they didn't have the effect she had expected. People couldn't resist turning the dial, and when they saw themselves as they would be at seventy, eighty, and ninety, something wonderful and extraordinary happened. While some were freaked out by their future saggy, wrinkly selves, most realized that they looked just like their Grandma Jean or their Grandpa George and found a new connection with and compassion for their older relatives. It turned out that the dials went the other way too, so that older folks could show the younger set how they looked when they were their age. It was a much more powerful and awesome experience than looking at old photographs. Everyone was saying that Elvira Queen was a visionary for finding a way to "bridge the age divide" and showing the world that we are all the same.

Romy and I went back for one more visit to Madame Fredepia, but she and all traces of her fortune-telling/ spell-selling business were gone. In its place there was a regular-looking yoga studio. I was disappointed because even though Madame Fredepia had kind of started the whole mess, she had meant to help me and Mom, and I wanted to tell her how things had turned out. And also, it would have been really nice to hear her say, *Well done.*

I've collected all of Mom's books to read over the school break, and Romy says she'll help me because there are a lot of them and most are not what you'd call page-turners. *Damsels in Discourse: An Analysis of the Princess Archetypes* and *The False Feminism of Disney Villains* aren't the type of books I'd usually pick up. Maybe they'll be horribly boring, but I'm hoping that I'll find out more about magic—not the dangerous stuff that Mom warned me about (I'm guessing she wouldn't put that in a book anyway), but something that will help me understand what happened to me. Knowing that there is magic all around us and that we share our world with ambitious fairy-tale villains, princesses who are stuck on a hamster wheel of marriage proposals and weddings, and fairy godmothers—some of them fully paid-up members of the League and some of them rogue members like Madame Fredepia—seems really amazing and sort of wonderful. But it also seems a little scary. I don't know whether or not I'll wake up on my twentieth birthday and look thirty—Mom says that won't happen because I broke the counterspell without using the Evil Queen's magic, and I hope she's right—or whether or not the Sea Witch still wants to turn me into a mermaid.

Romy keeps telling me that there's nothing to worry about. The Sea Witch is in jail and the Evil Queen's on her way to Norway to pick up the Nobel Peace Prize. They have bigger things to worry about than my legs and youthful complexion.

I hope Romy's right.

But a girl can't help but worry.

Acknowledgments

Thank you to my wonderful agent, Claire Anderson Wheeler. Your input made this book so much better, and your warmth and unfailing good humor made the publishing process a delight.

Thank you to everyone at Simon & Schuster, Aladdin. I am especially grateful to my editor, Jessica Smith, whose incredible eye for detail, wit, and emotion took this book to a new level. Special shout-outs for Karin Paprocki and Sara Mensinga for the incredible cover. Mike Rosamilia, the interior designer who made the pages of this book look so beautiful. Christina Solazzo, the managing editor who kept everything and everyone on schedule. Sara Berko, production manager who oversaw the nuts and bolts of making this book. Nicole Valdez, publicist. Kathleen Smith and Nicole Tai, proofreaders. Rebecca Vitkus, copyeditor extraodinaire who spotted, among other things, that Cia's middle school schedule didn't make any sense. Anna Parsons, Aladdin editor who gave the manuscript another read and its author much encouragement.

Thank you to my incredible daughters. My first readers: Kate, Maeve, Evie, and Rose. I am grateful every day for the four of you. Your joy, sense of humor, and allround brilliance inspires me to be a better writer and human being.

Thank you to my amazing parents, Mary and Brendan O'Neill; my hilarious and uber-talented sisters, Ellie O'Neill and Niamh O'Neill; and the world's best big brother, Shane O'Neill. Warmest thanks to my lovely in-laws, Krishna and Mohinder Kadyan.

A huge thank you to the dear friends who read early drafts of *The Princess Revolt*. Your insightful questions and enthusiasm gave me the support I needed to keep going. Cathy and Riley Andrews; Nicole and Priya Julian; Jodi, Sophia, and Lila Holland; Finley Ahearn; and Clara Shaw.

And, finally, thank you to my one-in-a-million husband, Vinny. None of this would have been possible without you. It was your work, support, and example that made it possible for me to pursue my dream. I can never thank you enough.